The Amazing adventures of Roy Hicks

A Novel by Nalle Windahl

The second book in the Saga Quadrology

First edition

Förlag: BoD – Books on Demand, Stockholm, Sverige
Tryck: BoD – Books on Demand, Norderstedt, Tyskland

ISBN: 978-91-7969-955-0

This page has been left blank intentionally. But these words have also been placed here intentionally, so this is no longer a blank page. It is the blank page paradox.

Book cover

Yet again, I am proud to say that Patrik Åkervinda has provided the image on the cover. Like always, please use the magic of internet to find him and more of his work if you are interested!

Find out more

And as before, check out my webpage for news, more information, and perhaps some extra material.

https://jnw.se

Disclaimer

I would reuse the same disclaimer as I did in the first book, but figured, it is already in writing there, so you can just read it there... and if you do not have access to a copy right now, there is no need to worry, it is not the most important part of the book, so just carry on an please enjoy this book as well!

A thank you!

Thank you!

Summary of the first book in this quadrology:

(spoiler warning if you have not read the first book just yet!)

Dee, a young girl, defies her father and escapes the safety of her village to get down to the harbour camp to meet up with her brother who is expected to return. The ship, the Glory, were lost at sea in an attack by sea monsters. One crewman survived and secured the cargo, a giant silver egg.

As Dee makes her way through the forest in the direction towards the harbour camp, she gets lost in a mysterious mist, created by the evil wizard Leola. In the mist Dee is trapped in the middle of a fight between vampires and werewolves but manages to escape. During her escape she falls down in the Sorrow, a ravine created by the strange creature Groll, a troll, who grieves the loss of his beloved Rueen, a long, long time ago. Rueen was killed by black witches, and due to that, Groll has lost his faith in humanity. Even so, he helps Dee get out of the ravine. On their way they find another survivor from the Glory, Tadao.

Dee, Groll and Tadao meet Leola, who does not reveal her true intentions and joins them as they make their way back to the harbour camp, for Dee to re-join with her father.

Upon their return to Dee's village they find it attacked and lost to enemy hands, and they are taken captivity. Only to escape during an attack by the undead. Saved by a youngster on the sky road along with a new friend, the dwarf Veron. They later take the sky road to the mountains in the east to track the other survivor of the Glory, and possibly the cargo.

Veron left the dwarf society after Grand Master Phidas mysteriously disappeared from the main dwarf society. Veron got the "honour" to lead the delegation to bring the news to king Thidas, the self-claimed ruler of the northern dwarf province. King Thidas is obsessed to reunite the legendary stones, and by taking control of the main mines he is certain to obtain his goal. Veron's nephew is caught in the middle of old secrets, old clan politics and the new order that king Thidas forces on the entire population in the main mines. But with his different way of seeing things and thinking, he gets a big and important position in this new order.

Grand Master Phidas, the rightful ruler of the main mines, left on a quest to destroy the vampires who he regretted helping a long time ago. On his way he meets the questionable Roy Hicks, a thief, hustler and liar that has been thrown out of his own town and is declared an outcast. Roy helps Phidas on his mission and they meet a girl that seems rather acquainted with Roy, even if he does not know her at all, Yena. She invites Roy and Phidas back to her house where her lover, Vladir, a vampire, who celebrates their arrival with a meal and shows them the sky road. Roy and Phidas uses the sky road to get to their goal, ending the vampires. After completing their mission, they take the sky road to join the other dwarf that also happens to walk the sky road at the same time.

The two dwarves leave the sky road to try and go back to dwarf society and try to prevent king Thidas on his quest to rule the entire dwarf society.

The vampires caught a werewolf in the fight where Dee managed to escape. Their prisoner, a grey witch called Grime, harness the power of the werewolf and enhances the vampire ruler who has already been given extra gifts and powers by others. In the process Grime is forced to take the lives of innocent girls, and doing so, he crosses the thin line and starts his journey to a black witch. During the process, he finds out that his sister, Leola, has done something terrible to him in the past.

The other surviving crewman from the Glory, who secured the cargo, guarded by what seems to be just about every werewolf, turns out to be Rick, Dee's brother. And as Dee and the others unite with Rick on the mountain Leola reveals her true intentions. Groll is badly harmed, but he awaits the arrival of Roy, to give him a small piece of the cargo the Glory carried. The rest Groll gives Dee, making her the last white witch.

An old friend comes to say goodbye to Groll, and as he vanishes, so does Roy. And there they are, on the mountainside, Dee, Rick and Tadao.

Dialog after the adventures

On the mountaintop, just above a steep edge, on a little rock sat a human being so still and so steady that if someone had passed, they might have stopped a while to take a look at the beautiful statue that someone oddly had placed here.

If they had looked closely, they would see that moss had gotten grip of the statue, and tiny pieces of grass has started to grow on top of the feet of the statue.

Even so, it seemed so real and almost like it was lightly and slowly breathing.

And it was. It was no statue, it was a man waiting, a man who had been waiting for an exceptionally long time. Sitting, at the same spot, day and night, summer and winter. A man who longed to get back to where he once left, long time ago from his perspective, but in a future slowly closing from the perspective of others.

Out of nowhere, another man appeared behind the waiting man, and the newcomer took a few steps towards the waiting man and sat next to him on the ground.

"Beautiful view you have chosen! This is indeed a place to wait for time to pass!"

The waiting man slowly turned his head, using muscles he had not used in several seasons. Blinked with his eyes a few times, again, something he had not done in an exceptionally long time.

"I did not expect to see you again!"

"Nor I you, but Groll wanted something different. He always has a way of getting his wishes through."

"How did you find me, and why?" The waiting man asked the newly arrived, much larger man.

10

"Ah, questions for later, my friend. And yes, you are my friend. A friend of Groll is a friend of mine."

"In that case, friend, who are you? And how can you disappear and then reappear at another place in another time?"

"I am one of the four wizards of old. This is our universe. We... administer and manage everything around you, even further than your eyes can see..."

"If that was your answer and explanation it was a poor one. As a friend, I ask you to answer in a way that I can understand."

"Well, you see, it is hard to explain, because you lack some important points of reference that you need to fully comprehend who I am. But let's try and break down the question. You say I disappear and reappear in different places at different times..."

The waiting man nodded, still looking out at the view.

"Let's say you had a thousand cows. All born a day a part. Then you would have a cow that was one day old and your oldest would be a thousand days old. Then let's say you take all your cows, put them in a long line, the oldest first, and the youngest last. All standing in the same direction looking at the sunrise. If you walked away from them to a point where you could turn around and look at all the thousand cows simultaneously. If they all looked the same it would be as you looked at the same cow, a thousand times, in different stages of its life. That is kind of how I see the world. I see everything, not only the space and dimensions surrounding you, but also where you are in time. So, if I want to visit you as the one-day old cow. I appear next to the one-day old cow. If I want to visit you as the hundred-day old cow. I appear next to the hundred-day old cow."

"So you see things in a different way?"

"Yes, a much different way. And to make it even more complicated, when you imagined the thousand cows, I told you to picture them in a row. But in reality, each living thing is moving, even the things you see as still, like trees, mountains, the ocean, your entire world is moving along with every star in the sky, the sun, your moons…"

"Speaking of moons… I am waiting for the two red moons to rise, then I know it's time…"

"Curious… tell me more…"

"Well, when I first met Groll and Rueen, or rather, when I met them, ah, you know, I met Groll alone first, then he gave me the life essence, but then I followed you and I ended up much earlier, and when I met Groll and Rueen at that time, there were two silver moons. And when I grew up, there was one silver moon and one blood moon. So, when I first saw the two silver moons, I knew something were different… and when Rueen… when she… well, that is when the first moon turned red. So I figure, when the second moon turns red, that is when he is gone. That is my cue to go back to Phidas and the others."

"Ah, so ages of life have made you more experienced and thoughtful. Great insight regarding the moons… and you know, when we are done talking, I will go to Groll and say goodbye. Tonight, is the first time this world will see two blood moons…"

"So my wait is over?"

"It is over when you choose that it is over… but if you are waiting for the blood moons, then yes, it is soon over…"

"This is rather rare, isn't it?"

"What do you mean?"

"You, talking with someone like me…"

"Yes, it is… but Groll and Rueen were my friends. You were important to them. So, I honour them. And besides…"

The Wizard did not continue…

"With the cows you answered how you found me, but you have not answered why… So, I assume that the 'besides' would be followed with the 'why' but it is something you already know, and I don't, and it is not something that I am supposed to know yet, since it, from my perspective, not have happened yet…"

"Yes, something like that…"

Both men sat silent a while, admiring the view and the sun as it slowly moved over the sky.

"Tell me a story, Roy Hicks, you have lived for ages and have seen and heard more than any other living being in this world so far. I bet you have more than one story to share."

Meeting a dragon according to Roy

"Well, the first thing that happened when you disappeared was ending up at the same place I was at before I got lost in time. Of course, I did not realize that at the moment, from my perspective everybody was gone, and somehow, I was at the same spot, but everything looked different.

I turned around to see if I could get a glimpse of any of the others, or quite frankly, terrified to find any of the werewolves that had all disappeared over the edge and into a valley ahead."

Roy looked around and pointed.

"It must have been that valley over there… anyway, I thought that perhaps the others had entered the cave, even if I thought it would be strange. That was the only reasonable thing I could come up with at the time, I mean, people don't just disappear… except you that is…"

Roy started to move his arms and legs, as if trying to wake up his body.

"When I entered the cave, I realized two things, I was not alone and my company was not the ones I expected."

Roy started gesturing with his arm, a little uncontrolled at first, but pretty soon he had regained control of his arms.

"Right before me was a huge face of horrible fire breathing dragon. She guarded her small offspring that looked like small worms. Or rather, small compared to their mother. She stared straight into my eyes, and smoke came out of her mouth and she inhaled as if she were about to turn me into a human torch…."

Roy's gestures seemed rehearsed, as if he had told the tale of the dragon a hundred times before.

"But I looked right back in her eyes, and she turned her head away, letting out a small flame that heated a small area beside her. I think she had to let out her steam, so it would not consume her as she apparently did not dare touch me. The area started to melt and glow, leaving everything behind it even darker than before."

Roy looked over at the wizard to see if he was following his story.

"Then, without warning, a couple of smaller creatures crawled out from under her. They looked almost like earth worms, only bigger. It was hard to tell, since it was so dark behind the whole, but at least two, maybe three worms dug their way through the hole and disappeared under ground. Then the dragon, out of fear for me, crawled backwards, further into the cave."

Roy could really feel the life returning to his body. He even started to feel hungry. Which of course was completely natural, since he had not eaten in a very, very long time.

"I could see small flames from the dragons nose moving further and further back to the point where the tiny dragon-flames was drowned by the glowing light from the whole."

Roy paused.

"That's the story when I scared away the dragon."

He sat quiet a long time again, then added thoughtfully.

"I visited the cave again before I decided to wait here. And it is not as deep as I remembered it. Really strange!"

The wizard only smiled, he knew that this was only a tale that Roy told, the real thing was a completely different version.

Meeting a dragon in reality

Roy did walk into the cave. Roy did meet a dragon. But the mother dragon looked at a paralyzed being and determined that this puny creature was not a threat to her or her offspring, thus leaving it be.

As she took a breath to preheat the ground for her little one's so they could safely dig their way through the mountain and enjoy it's protection until they had matured and grown enough to crawl out of the mountain and pupate only to hatch yet again, fully fledged dragons.

As she started to move further back into the cave, three of her offspring quickly crawled down into the mountain. The mother dragon returned to the two remaining hatched worms and the dozen unhatched eggs.

Roy could not move again until the fear that had paralyzed him had loosened its grip enough to allow him to slowly back out of the cave. And that happened a long while after he could no longer see her glowing breath in the dark.

It was only when Roy had managed to put a full days half running, half walking as he could relax and let what had happened sink in. Up until then, he was certain that he had never been as afraid as he was that day.

Dialog I

"Well, Roy, seems like you made quite an impact on the dragon, showing her who was in charge." The wizard laughed a little to himself.

"Nah, to be honest, I think it was really her that made the most impact. But you asked for a story, and a story you got!"

"Indeed I did! And we got plenty time to spare, from your perspective. And I have not planned anything else, so if you don't mind, I'll keep keeping you company until it's time for you to get moving. And I'd love to hear more stories!"

"A question before I tell another story. I got plenty. If you can visit time and space as you please, and see everything, there is really no point for me telling stories, are there? Because you already know what has happened or what will happen?"

"No, not really. There is almost never a point. And there is almost always a point. In this case there is no point. But most of the time the point is the choice. The choice you make, or don't make, is what affects the events to come. And you are equally affected by choices that are already made, or not made, both by you and others, now living and those who have lived before you. This time your choice to entertain me with stories from your long life will only amuse me or not amuse me, but in the whole, this is a rare moment where your choice will not affect anything surrounding you, as where most of your other choices have, and will continue to change the events to come."

"So, what you are saying is that all my choices so far has taken me, and possibly others, to this point in time, from my perspective, and this unique moment will not affect the future in any way?"

"Yes, and no. Your own choices, or lack of choices, always affect at least yourself. Like a thought for example. If you have thought of something, it is active in your mind, and what has once been active in your mind it can transform into reality. But as long as you have not had the thought, you can never make it real."

"So, if I choose to tell you stories, it will not affect the future, but it will affect my future version of myself, who can make different choices based on what I choose to do today?"
"Well put, and yes, it is true. And one thing that you forgot, it will also affect me and decide whether I will get entertained today or not."

"Ok, interesting thoughts! But I am not the one who have ever turned down a chance to tell a story. Is there something in particular you want to hear?"

"There are many stories I would like to hear, but first I would like to hear something that is not stories. I want to hear your reasoning behind three particular choices you have made…"

"What choices are you thinking about?"

"I am thinking about the choice to approach and follow me on the day Groll died, or rather, today when he will die, a choice that has caused a lot of change in this world. And I would like to hear the reasoning behind why you chose to buy and place the blast stones and firestones around the castle as you did, and when you did. And certainly not least, why you built the sky road."

First choice

"My first choice was not really a choice, it was more curiosity. I had seen the house appear out of thin air, you, walking out of it, both you and the house disappear again, without leaving any trace behind."

"Yes, ah, the house hidden in time and space, not my most cleaver decisions ever. Inside all rooms always change position, so there is no telling of what is behind each door. So I had been trapped inside that house for a very long while when you saw me exit it!"

"This is something you need to tell me more about, but now I am telling you about my first choice."

"Yes, sorry, continue please!"

"I later met Phidas, and sort of expecting him to vanish as well, only he did not. And then I did not think any further of it until you appeared on the mountain that day, or this day. So, it was kind of reassuring to see you again, that meant that I had not made you up or was crazy. And my curiosity took over. Simple as that. Not really a choice."

"Ah, but you see, there is always a choice, so what was the choice that the other you will make later today?"

"It was a long time ago, and I do not really recall all the details. But if I am correct, I will be thinking in the lines: Here is someone who I do not know who apparently knows me by name and was expecting me. He died. Err, will die. Phidas had found, eh, will find a fellow dwarf, the others I did not know, but felt some kind of connection to. Groll filled me with some silver thing making me almost immortal and then you came in the middle of everything. I figured that you were something that I could almost relate to, and my choice was to see if you could provide me with some answers. Why did people recognize me, what was the silver thing, and what was up with all the werewolves? It's tricky with the time reference, what has been even if it occurs in the future."

"You'll get used to it... so, what was the choice you made?"

"The choice? I chose to find answers, and I thought you would be the best way of getting those answers!"

"Exactly! That was the choice! Now, did you find your answers?"

"Well, no, I could not find you when you disappeared. And I did not know that I also disappeared. From my perspective both you and the others disappeared."

"So you are telling me you do not know the answers to your three questions?"

"Yes I do, to all three of them, but it was not you who answered them."

"Ah, so you expected to hear the answers from me? Well, that is not always the case. But you did get your answers. So, would you say it was a good choice?"

"Well, yes and no. If you define a good choice with an expected outcome, then yes, in a way. But it was not at all in the way I expected."

"There you have another interesting thing, a choice, or the lack of a choice, may not always get the expected result the expected way, but there will always be a result in one way or another."

"I've been thinking. You are the creator, aren't you?"

"Yes and no. From your perspective, Groll and Rueen are the creator, or rather, the creators. And from that same perspective, I would be the creator of your creators. So, I am a creator in a way, but not the way you mean when you speak of the creator, because you lack the general perspective to even think that there could be a creator of the creator... So, from your perspective I am a non-existent nobody... Now, what about the second choice?"

Second choice

"My second choice?"

"Yes, blast stones and fire stones at the castle..."

"Yes, that... well this is something that still makes me dizzy when I think about it. Counting from when I was born, I lived my life for many winters, until the day I saw you and met Phidas. That was a day were the first part of my life ended and the second part of my life started. During this second part, I experienced the destruction of the vampire castle, by Phidas' and my hands. And I experienced the sky road, how it was built and what its purpose was. Or rather, a few of many purposes. The rest I was told by people who already knew me but who was perfectly strangers to me at the time."

"Vladir and Yena?"

"Yes, among others... and they knew, because I had told them, from their perspective, that there would come a day when I would meet them for my first time, from my perspective, without any knowledge of everything. And as I told them, they did not tell or show me much, but enough."

"Enough for what?"

"Enough for me to know what to do when I got the chance to prepare things so I could do them later, even if later was first in my experience."

"So what about the blast stones and firestones?"

"Well, I first went there to check out the surroundings, and could not find any traces of blast stones or firestones. And then I thought that they might have gotten there from when they constructed the castle, you see, it was not built yet when I was there the first time, or rather, the second time, but still before everything."

"I can understand how it makes you dizzy…"

"And then I visited it a third time, after the castle was built, but still no traces of the blast stones or the fire stones."

"So you made it happen?"

"Yes, I was afraid that without the stones, Phidas and I would not be able to blow the castle up, so I bought all the necessary things from the dwarves shortly after they had opened up for trading and arranged for them to be placed outside the castle once it had been abandoned by its first owners and before the vampires took it as their strong hold."

"And what would you say your choice was in this?"

"My choice? Well…" Roy had to think for a minute. "…I think my choice was to make sure I could repeat what I had already done. I figured that since I have already done it, it needs to be done again, by Phidas and me. If not, what would happen to me here? Would I still end up here or would this enchantment be broken, and I would never had ended up here in the first place?"

"Interesting point of view, I did not see that coming!"

Third choice

"And I guess that is true for my third choice as well, the sky road I mean…"

"So, by repeating what you knew would happen, making sure it really would happen again, without knowing any impact of not doing them, or by doing them for that matter, your choices was to recreate what you knew was true from your memory of the things you had experienced a long time ago, from your perspective, yet things that had not yet occurred from everyone else's perspective?"

"Yes, that is a way to put it, I guess… I mean, what would happen if I did not repeat it? Would I still be here? Would I still be me?"

"Yet you do not know the future from this point on, a future you have helped create by recreating things from your memory? Do you know the consequences of your actions in building the sky road and blowing up the castle?"

"No, I just know that I did it… so I figured it needed to be done… Was that wrong?"

"Yes and no… it was your choices, choices that affect the outcome of many things in this world, both in the past, now and in the future. A big disturbance of the expected chain of events in this world…"

The wizard looked at Roy's puzzled face expression and laughed out loud.

"Don't worry Roy! You are not the only one who have affected the expected chain of events in this world. Or in any world for that matter. Things rarely go as expected. There is always the aspect of life finding its own way through time, from your perspective."

"But if you can see everything as a series of events in time, can you not see what will happen here in the future and is not everything already decided?"

"Well, again, yes and no! Everything is already decided. And I can see everything. But the future, from your perspective, changes when someone makes an unexpected decision. That happens all the time, but mostly with little things. Once and a while, someone makes a decision that has major impact of the future, from your perspective."

"How come you cannot see it?"

"Well, in order to see everything I need to look the whole time, and then I see everything, including what you call the future. But not even I can pay attention to everything all the time. As soon as I look away and pay attention at something else, a little choice can change everything. And when I look back, there is a new version of the things I saw earlier. Then the previous thing only exists in my mind."

"But what if you decide to visit a place in the future, and then go back in time again, can that future be changed based on different decisions that are being made through out time?"

"Well, to explain that I need to make two things clear and point out that I do not expect you to fully understand. First thing I like to point out is that in a universe, such as this where this planet orbits around a sun and two moons orbit the planet, and where the universe is filled with different suns and planets, in fact, every star you see on the night sky is a sun with planets orbiting it. Now in every universe, time is a factor or a dimension, in what occurs in that specific universe. And with the factor of time, the universe is true and solid. But both without the factor time, and with the factor of choice, each universe, there are plenty of those you know, becomes a part in the multiverse. And just to mess it up, there are plenty of multiverses as well… And the multiverses my friend, that's my arena, and that is where I move through time and space…"

The wizard looked at Roy, and it was obvious that Roy did not get what he just said.

"I warned you that you would not understand. But let it sink in and give it time, perhaps even choice, and then it might clear eventually."

Roy just kept looking at the view without saying anything.

"Say something Roy, or else I am afraid that I broke you, and if so, I need to fix you somehow... because you have a part in the future as well..."

Roy still did not say anything.

"Tell me another story Roy. Tell me about when you met the sea folk!"

Meeting the Sea Folk according to Roy

"Well, when I had spent a long time with Groll and Rueen I had heard them talk about the Sea Folk. From what I understand, they did not create the Sea Folk, someone before them did that, and now I suppose that someone is you?"

"Yes, I created the Sea Folk by accident. But nevertheless, it was me."

"Then I would like to hear that story from you later!"

"We'll see about that, now continue, please…"

"Ok. When we parted ways, I was curious of what the Sea Folk was, and since Groll told me that I could not drown, I decided to try it, so I started with dipping my head in a bucket of water and hold my breath for as long as I could, and when I could not hold it any longer, I panicked and pulled my head up again. And then I did not do anything more for about two full moon cycles. Then I decided that I had to have faith in Groll, so I took, literally, a leap of faith and found myself a cliff over the ocean and jumped in. Only on my way down I regretted it, since I had no idea how deep the water was beneath me, but then it was too late. Fortunate for me, it was deep enough and as I fell through the air, and down under the surface, I kind of let whatever would come happen to me."

Roy was on track again, and the Wizard was relieved that he in fact did not break Roy, and he still would have the possibility to play his part in all that was about to come.

"Once under water, a new world opened up to me. New type of growing things, large and small, new life forms, mostly fish, crabs and squids, and in my surprise of all marvellous things I forgot that I was under water. The first thing that occurred to me was that it was difficult, but not impossible, to walk under water. The second thing was an amazement that I could see so clear under water. I remember when I grew up and took a swim in a lake or a river,

27

even if the water looked crystal clear from above, it was impossible to see much under water, but now, I could see as if I was at land. The third thing that came to me was the breathing. I could breath as easy as I can on dry land. An amazing experience all together. And I do not know for how long I was walking the bottom of the ocean before I first came across the Sea Folk. But I know it was several days and several nights."

Roy had almost a million stars glittering in his eyes as he told this story.

"When I first saw them, there were only a few, they did not see me, but I followed them as best as I could. I could not walk as fast as they could swim, so I only followed them from a general direction. And when I came to their city, they welcomed me with open arms and thought I was the most interesting creature that they had ever encountered. They took me straight to their king and he made me a guest of honour at the festivities they held that night. I later learned that the celebration was in my honour since I made such a deep impression on them."

Again, the wizard laughed quietly to himself.

Meeting the Sea Folk in reality

Roy did see only a few Sea Folk at first, but they also saw him and instantly fled from him, not because the thought he looked dangerous, but because they do not like to interact with humans.

They tried to lose him by swimming in different directions and made sure that the human lost all track of them, and away from their nearby outskirt villages and the brink of their entire society. But somehow the stupid human got terribly lost by losing their trails and did not seem to be able to navigate by the sky, so eventually he found his way to their main city where the entire Royal family lived.

He was immediately captured when crossing the outer border to their city and brought directly to an emergency trial where it was decided that he would be sacrificed to the great sea monster. The only one who opposed this was the king's youngest daughter, Arell. She demanded that the strange human would be given a weapon to give him a chance against the horrid creature.

So, the king decided that he would get one of their traditional weapons, a trident. Arell was pleased with this, even if she thought that the strange man still did not stand a chance. But at least it felt more just to give him a one in a million chance of surviving, than no chance at all.

Creating the Sea Folk

"Now I have told you a story, it is your turn. How did the Sea Folk come to be?" Roy asked the wizard.

"A long and complicated story, but the short and simple version of it is something like this... After this planet was created, there was no moons, no life. And the first time I visited it, I did not like the life that was here. So, I attempted to destroy it by flooding the whole valley."

"Wait, you said that when the planet was created there was no life, and the first time you visited here was life, how did life come to be?"

"That was something I created the second time I was here, and remember, I do not experience the factor time as you do. When I flooded the valley, my ambition was to start over from scratch, recreating life without any other influences. So, after the flood I created the trolls out of rocks, and I watched them thrive until I found Groll and Rueen, then I made them creators of this world. But what I failed to realize when I flooded the valley is that life itself is adaptive and very keen on keep living. So the first and most obvious thing that happened was that some of the first people on this planet survived the flood and drifted on the ocean to other landmasses in the ocean. The second thing that happened was totally unpredictable. Here was sea life in the oceans before the flood, and by chance one particularly mother-to-be of a nasty sea monster happened to feed on three different beings, one land living person that saw swept out to sea, one very intelligent spices of mammal fish and a type of frog that had also been swept out to sea. The foetuses of the mother to be gained all kinds of traits from the food their mother just consumed, and when they were born, they were the first of their kind. Part human, part fish, part frog and part sea monster. Or as you call them, the Sea Folk."

"Huh. Sounds simple enough, mix a couple of different creatures and create a new. But how come that it does not happen to others, how come a pregnant wolf who eats a cow, or a horse still get baby cubs?"

"That particular sea monster was a template for other monsters, and her foetuses were in a particularly critical stage of their development and was perceptive to the change that their mother's food provided. I honestly don't know what caused it, but I am guessing that the frog was a vital part of what took place. The frog was also a sort of template creature, and a creature that is very adaptive to its surroundings. But it is only a guess."

"Another thing, you said there are more landmasses in the ocean, and other people that survived the flood. Are they like us?"

"Exactly the same, only evolved many, many, many more ages than your spices have."

"How come you created the same people again if you felt like destroying the first once you created?"

"I didn't create the same people again, you did."

A long quiet paus emerged.

"What do you mean that I created the same people again?"

"By inspiring Groll and Rueen."

"But how can I inspire them to create the same people again when I was born ages after they created the first of the current people? Or did they create the current people? I mean, how can I, a son of the current people inspires creation of the other people that existed before the current people?"

"Time is a complex dimension, and the multiverses are an even more complex creation. Now, tell me another story from your time with the sea folk!"

Becoming a Sea God according to Roy

"You know, when I left them, I was raised to some sort of Sea God."

"A Sea God you say? How did that happen?"

"At the party they threw for me, they gave me a kind of weapon and showed me a path leading away from their city. It was the strangest looking spear I have ever seen, longer than me and instead of one pint at the end it split up in three sharp end points. After I started walking, it did not take long until a huge Sea creature came towards me. Of course, I was a bit terrified at first, but then I remembered my encounter with the dragon, and figured that I could handle this creature as well. I only rose my spear and scared away the creature and never saw it again. When I looked back towards the city, I saw them charging and celebrating. So, I walked back towards them."

"Scaring away a big Sea Monster, that is something…" the wizard could almost not hide his laughter, but Roy continued as if he had not been interrupted or heard the laugh and did not seem to be offended in anyway.

"I did not come far before their leader came out to greet me. Two of his guards posted in front of me, crossing their spears to block my path back. Their leader took of his crown, or at least that's what I think it was, a primitive ring of some underwater vegetation. He put it on my head. Neither of them spoke to me, but still I understood that he crowned me, and sent me away to chase down the sea monster and relieve them of their threat. Apparently impressed with my handling of the first encounter. So, I could not do anything else than embrace their celebration and coronation to some kind of protective God."

By now the wizard's body was clearly bobbing up and down due to his asphyxiated laughter.

"I turned around again and left them, only never to return. I thought best to leave them be, at peace and not interact with them too much. I never had any intention of disturbing their way of life, and by a short encounter like I had, and getting celebrated as a Sea God I figured it was best to leave them alone all together."

The wizard could not hold back his laughter anymore, and burst out into an open, almost uncontrolled loud laugh.

"You do tell great and entertaining stories, my dear Roy!" he managed to declare between his shortness of breath and more laughs lining up in his throat waiting for the first opportunity to escape out in the open.

Becoming no Sea God at all in reality

What really happened was a different story all together. After banishing Roy and sacrificing him to the sea monster that lured in the outskirts of their territory. They did not expect that the creature would lure so close. So, with cries, equal of surprise, fear and hope that the creature would tear the odd land creature apart, the entire sea folk population managed to scare the sea monster on the run, temporarily. Later is would return for a fatal attack. But for now, the sea monster ran off to hide and wait. As the sea monster vanished, the odd land creature seemed to return. So, the king himself swam out to show him that he was no longer welcome. And as he approached the oddity, he figured that he might want some gift or some other token, and the only thing he could think of was his crown. Each morning he got a freshly made crown of the season's finest plants and seaweed. Every night the crown was released in a current, giving it back to the sea. But today, he gave it to the odd land creature instead. The sea folk later took the 'not returning the crown to the sea' as the reason for the attack of the great sea monster, which of course had nothing to do with the attack, it was only their superstition playing them a game. The sea creature had attacked either way, and with great loss among the sea folk, they managed to slay the sea monster and put its huge and massive body on poles as a warning to other sea monsters. Except for its eyes, they were sacrificed with the crown to the current that very same night. It turned out that the engagement with the sea monster totally clouded the meeting with Roy, and he was completely forgotten and did not end up in the sea folk history scrolls, except for one sentence:
"Our great king gave his crown to a stranger the day before the attack, and because of that, the sea monster attacked us the very next day."
The sentence that followed was a rule that the sea folk made sure never to break again:
"That is why our great king has strictly forbidden any contact with outsiders for all future."

Guarding the sea folk according to Roy

"Not bad," the wizard said laughing. "becoming a Sea God with only a small encounter like that! Did you spend any more time with the sea folk?"

"No, I figured it was best leaving them alone, try not to influence them too much with my God-like presence. But I wandered the sea floor looking for dangers that could cause potential threats to the sea folk. Do you know how big the sea floor really is? It took me forever to wander around trying to cover as much territory as I possibly could."

"Indeed, it is a big world beneath the surface, a very rich world with a lot of species and dangers of all kinds.

"No, I found it rather peaceful and maybe even a bit dull. Most of all very vast."

"So, you did not see any other creatures down there?"

"Well, mostly fish, and occasionally a sea monster at a distance, but I was surprised how little life there really are at the bottom of the sea."

"Strange that you say this, I always figured that the sea is rich with life…" the wizard laughed again, clearly amused by Roy and his different views and stories.

"Yes, and after a great while, I figured the sea floor was fairly safe and that the sea folk were not in any danger that they would not manage by themselves. So, I decided to go back up to dry land again."

Roy paused a bit, as if to try to think of what to say next.

"Only problem was that I had been down under for so long that I had totally lost my bearing, and when I got up on dry land again, it took a while to realise that I was nowhere near the land I had left. Turned out there are more dry land in this world, perhaps even more dry land than ocean. I found twenty-three pieces of land before I returned to familiar shorelines. And even then, I was not completely sure that I was on the right place, it had changed a lot over the years."

"I can imagine, time does that to land."

"That was about it when it comes to my time under water. And once back on dry land, it took quite a long time to readjust for land conditions and breathing air again…"

Guarding the sea folk in reality

Now, what really happened was more like this. Even if Roy tried to find his way back to the sea folk, he never managed to find them again, despite years and years of searching. During his search Roy did not see as much of the sea life as one would expect, mostly since all sea life could sense his presence and fled upon his arrival to their domain. Roy did not fit in to either known predator nor known food and to most sea life that meant stay away. On occasion Roy had seen sea monsters at a distance, but he was a lucky bastard and each and every time he got close to a sea monster, they were distracted by a bigger target. And despite Roy's assumption that there was little life beneath the surface, and that the sea folk were in no danger, they were always in danger. Mostly from the big variety of sea monsters, but that was only one of many dangers they faced.

And when Roy decided to abandon his search for the sea folk and make his way back to dry land, he was lost and tried to systematically try each direction to find land again. Mostly he was unlucky and missed it, despite his many tries. And of the twenty-three landmasses he claimed to have discovered, he only visited a total of six landmasses, but from different directions, one of them as many as fourteen times.

Little did he know that there were over forty larger landmasses on this world, and more than twice as many as smaller landmasses, but only two were inhabited (oddly enough both by descendants of Roy). And luck kept him companion most of the time, so he managed to finally find his way back to familiar land. To his defence it had changed a lot since he left it.

Dialog II

"This makes me curious. I have never been able to talk to a being that can live both in water and on land. How does the transaction from water to land feel? I can imagine the transaction from air to water and that the body is struggling as if it was drowning when the body adapts to breathing water instead of air. But I cannot imagine reverse drowning. How did that feel?"

Roy thought for a moment.

"It is like nothing I have ever experienced, so I cannot compare it to anything, and it is difficult to set words on. But have you ever been in a really cold environment, perhaps in the winter, and then in an instant you are suddenly indoors in a warm room or tent where a fire is raging and has been for a very long time, so that the air inside is so much warmer than the air outside?"

"Ah, you forget that I do not share your physiology, I do not live in time and space as you do, thus I am not bound by its laws. I can do what you would call breathing in mid space, lightyears away from the closest stars or planets where no air exists, and no matter nor gravitation is present."

"I will pretend that I understood what you just said and assume it means 'yes' and will continue like planned."

Both laughed out loud, a relieving laughter, even if there were no tension between the two, but still a laughter that somehow connected them in real friendship.

"Like I was saying, undrowning feels a little like when you replace the cold, freezing air from outside, with the overheated warm air from inside. And the way you need to do it, to get somewhere near the feeling in the lungs is to take a deep, deep breath outside, exhale as you enter the warm room and inhale again only as you stand next to the warming fire. This way your lungs and entire body is still cold and expect the cold, but instead of the expected cold air you send down raging warm air. This causes both a burning sensation in the lungs themselves, a very painful experience, and then the heat spreads quickly, first in your chest, then to your head and to all the other parts of your body. And that is how the inside of your body feels like. The outside of your body experiences the opposite journey. As if you were in a rather warm and comfortable environment only to all of a sudden arrive naked in a cold surrounding with no protection against the cold and nothing to give you any heat. As the mind experience both those contradictory feelings it starts sending mixed signals to your entire body, so both on the inside and outside you simultaneously feel warm and cold, and your body is on full alert and starts all system reactions to start to cool you and reheat you. Naturally, the pulse rises to increase the blood flow through all muscles throughout the entire body. Blood that carries both water and air. Confusing the body that is designed to either or, not both at the same time. And after just a few breaths the water is entirely purged from the lungs and the body starts to regulate normally again, resetting all active fail safes and alarm systems and then the body relaxes totally, as if it had been a little tense under water…"

"Sounds like a liberating feeling once it is done, and I will pretend that I understood what you just said and assume it means 'unpleasant' and will be satisfied with that short answer…"

Both laughed again, continuing to deepen their relationship.

"You are quite something, Roy! No wonder I keep meeting you everywhere and everywhen."

"Everywhen!? Is that even a word?"

"Yes, of course! Like everywhere describes any physical place, everywhen describes any place in time…"

"Perhaps it is why I have never heard it, I am not familiar with the time perspective…"

"Not yet, but you will be, my friend!"

"About that, what do you mean with all this? Will we meet again?"

"Many times, my friend. As we have already met many times, from this worlds timeline perspective."

"Yes, this is our third encounter…"

"Yes, counting from your current perspective, but counting from the birth of this world, we have met many, many times already… I even had to make up a new word to describe you!"

"A new word? How do you mean? A new word like everywhen?"

"No, nothing like everywhen, that is an established word. The new word I made up just for you is a time wanderer."

"That is two words."

"Ok, then I had to make up an entirely new expression. Time wanderer."

"Huh, time wanderer? Sounds like I have a lot to look forward to…"

"Yes, and back, if you use this worlds timeline…"

"You confuse me, old man!"

"I suppose, but it is important that you learn this now, at this stage in your journey. It will help a lot in your future, counting from your perspective!"

Roy sat quiet for a while, trying to grasp what he just had heard. It did not go so well.

"Did I tell you about the time where I sneaked passed the dwarf guards and entered their mine?"

"No, you have not, let's hear about it!"

When Roy snuck in the dwarf mine according to Roy

"It was before the old King Midas took the throne. I believe it was still his father Sephidas the reigned, but it had to be in the end of his regime. There were the usual posts at the gates to the mine, so getting through there was bound to fail. But I was curious and wanted to see how it looked inside. I had heard from one of my trading partners at the time, that the inside of the dwarf mines was decorated with the most precious metals and gemstones that they had found, and that everything was covered with magnificent sculptures sculptured direct into the mountain itself."

"Were they?"

"I'll get to that, first I want to tell you how I got in!"

"Sorry for interrupting, continue please!"

"As I said, coming through the main entrance to the mine were out of question. I had to find another way in. And I knew that in order to get air down to the mines, the dwarves had to have some sort of ventilation technology, or else they would suffocate down in their mines. If not only by breathing, then definitely with all the fires they had going to get the heat needed for much of their processing of ores, minerals and refined metals."

"Good thinking!"

"I had to search for a long while, because the dwarves are cleaver craftsmen and had concealed the air vents carefully. Crafted in a way to blend in with the surroundings, almost hidden to the naked eye. I had to use my sharp eyes to see small changes in the direction of the winds slowly moving over the mountain before I could find any air vent. And even when I had detected a shift in the air movements, it was hard to see the opening, I had to feel my way with hands and feet to be able to identify the opening itself. Once that was done, going down was easy. You know – dwarf feet and human feet are about the same size, which was very lucky for me.

They had carved steps all the way down to the mine tunnels, and the steps were small, but big enough for both dwarf feet and my feet, to be able to walk rather safely down. And when I got down to the tunnels, I got to experience the magnificence of the dwarf craftmanship. The tunnel I entered from the ventilation shaft was not one of the main tunnels, but they were still beautifully carved with smooth surfaces and sculptures here and there. I was so taken by the beauty that I forgot I had trespassed and walked around freely to admire it all. It was a guard that found me, and he escorted me to his superior who without hesitation showed me to the main entrance and threw me out. But along the way we passed many marvellous creations and I tried to get a glimpse of as many things that I possibly could."

"So, the dwarves had carved their art directly from the mountain?"

"Yes, indeed they had, but not everything. Some creations looked like they were placed there but created elsewhere."

"Even if I claim to have been everywhere and seen everything, I have never visited the dwarf mines. But I know I will, in the future, from your perspective. And on top of it all, I know I will be guided by you..."

"But I have only been there this one time, how can I possibly guide you?"

"Thing will fall into place when it is time..."

When Roy snuck in the dwarf mine in reality

As you probably know by now, not everything Roy says is as it really were. But it is true that Roy set out to find the entrance to the dwarf mine, but as he reached the end of the path where the entrance was supposed to be, he could not find it. And he wandered for days trying to locate it. And by chance, he stumbled on a ventilation shaft. But did not realize it at first and certainly did not discover it by will. He sat down to paus, and as he leaned back to rest against the mountain wall, the wall failed to catch him as he expected it to, and he fell head first down a long staircase carved directly into the mountain. It was when the stair took a rather sharp turn that Roy stopped falling and remained there still for a while before daring to move. At first, he could not decide if he would go back up or continue down. But he managed to make a sound decision and figured that if he continued down he would probably not find his way back, and he was curious to find out how he had missed the entrance that was obviously there. Sure, there were a slim chance that there was some kind of magic involved, thus not being able to find his way back down again. But the curiosity took over and he walked all the way back up and investigated the entrance he came through. And alas, he could use it to make his way back down. Roy figured that it had to be a ventilation shaft and that it was purposely built to be hard to see and by not seeing it, hard to find with a very low chance of uninvited guests using it. On his way back down again, he was very careful not to make a single sound and listened anxiously for any signs of movement ahead, but as soon as he came out in the first corridor of the mines and saw the first sculpture all his caution was gone in an instant and he laughed out loud to himself, and even cheered of his luck. And it was not very hard for the patrolling guard to hear Roy, nor identify where he was and quickly apprehend him and took him to is commander for a quick verdict of trespassing and thrown out of the main through the main entrance. And even if he were just thrown out through it, he could still not see it, even if he knew it was there. Probably concealed with the same brilliance as the ventilation shaft. And like that, he had managed to be thrown out of two different societies by two different spices.

Dialog III

"Even if I by now feel like I have known you for a long time, and perhaps I have, from your perspective, I still feel that there is much you have not told me, and perhaps you won't, but I kind of get the feeling that there is more than meets the eye with this visit of yours."

"Of course, you are right. As I said, I only visit you now because I will soon be visiting my dying old friend Groll, sorry, let me rephrase that, OUR old friend. But I decided to take the time to sit here with you since you have always fascinated me a great deal. You have, or rather will, from your perspective, gain a rather unique perspective on things. I created Groll, Groll created you giving you a kind of eternal life. I accidently gave you an ability to move across time. And what I am struggling with now is what I can tell you and what I cannot tell you. I figure that most of the things you will experience you will need to go through on your own to get to that unique perspective. And if I tell you things in advance, does that effect your experience and thus changing your experience and by doing so, changing the very future, from your perspective, because I have interfered."

"So, what you are saying is that you do not want to share things with me, kind of like Vladir and Yena?"

"Something to that extent, yes."

"I myself instructed Vladir and Yena not to tell my past self, from my perspective, anything about the future, from his perspective, because I too was worried what implications it may have, so I totally buy your point of view. And I will try to constrain my curiosity, but I need you to tell me one thing."

"I am not sure that I can, that entirely depends on what you ask of me..."

"Well, I kind of already have figured out a few things."

45

"And what would those be?"

"The first being that I am truly immortal and depending on my coming choices it may as well be that I will stay alive a long time, even affecting the outcome of the future."

"Nothing I am willing to confirm yet…"

"It's alright, just walk with me on this one. The second is that I have already affected the past, several times, but not the past from my perspective, but from this world's perspective. As so, I will need to travel through more of those time rifts, as I supposed they are."

"I'm with you and still listening…"

"The third thing is that everything has something to do with me, my views of things and my choices…"

"That it something I can confirm for you if you wish!"

"That is exactly my problem. You know who I am, right? Who I have been?"

"Yes, a liar, borderline thief and a most questionable honour!"

"My point exactly! I'm not somebody you can count or relay on. And if I know anything from my past is that the heroes of each and every story is honourable and just. And I'm not that guy."

"No, to that I can agree. But let me also put it like this:"

When Roy helped Rueen with the baby fox' according to the Wizard

"Do you remember one time when you helped Rueen with a pack of baby fox' that had lost their mother?"

"Yes, I do!"

"Then I will tell you what I saw, as an observer without any biased opinion of you, even without your own biased opinion…"

Roy turned his head to the Wizard curious to hear what he had to say.

"You see, it was you who first heard their little hungry cries. You made Rueen aware of the little creatures."

"Yes, that might be true, but it was Rueen that actually helped them, I did nothing to aid them."

"But you did, my friend. Yes, it was Rueen that used her special powers as a creator. She gave them the necessary life essence that accelerated their growth and knowledge, so they could manage by themselves. But do you know why she did it?"

"She, as well as I, was convinced that they would die if she did not act and did something to help them."

"Yes, that is correct. But as the creator she knew that life always needs to find its own way, for good and bad. A motherless pack of fox pups are meant to die. Either starve to death or be eaten by any number of predators that would find them a delicious meal."

"Stop! How can you say that? Now you are just being cruel!"

"No, that is nature being cruel, as nature is, and has to be. I am merely pointing out the course of nature. Underlining it to make my point."

"Which is? What is your point with this?"

"My point is that when Rueen saw you, and your affection towards these cute pups, she decided to break her code of conduct and intervein in natures harsh reality. She saw your vulnerability and by acting as she did, out of pity for you, she showed you how great caring for others really can be. Her affection for YOU saved those cubs. They continued to live because YOU cared."

"So, what you are saying is that Rueen helped those cubs because of me, and if I had not cared, she wouldn't have cared either?"

"Yes, that is right. You heard them, and even if you had not pointed it out, so would Rueen eventually. But she knew far too well that any intervention with the cause of nature could be devastating. As it was in this case as well… as always…"

"What do you mean devastating? All the pups survived. We saved them!"

"Yes, you did. And When Rueen used her life essence to help them grow, she chooses to sidestep the balance in many ways. And with those cubs she created a superior race of fox'. Now a days the original fox is extinct, and all foxes alive today is direct descendants of that brood."

"So, my caring for those pups, compassion if you may, altered the balance of life and had a serious impact of the future."

"Yes, spot on! And that is what makes you special. Many of your choices result in large changes of the worlds you visit, a small though or gesture that leads to great consequence. I have never seen anything like it in all the times, worlds and multiverses that I have in my spectre. Which makes you totally unique. Which you are even if you take away the fact that you cross every timeline in almost every multiverse. Most other living beings are lucky if one of their choices during their entire lifespan affects the world in the tiniest bit. But not you, you leave changes behind all the time and everywhere."

"That last part was nothing I understood."

"A good thing, I might have said just a bit too much."

When Roy helped Rueen with the baby fox' according to Roy

"The way I remember it, it was not a big deal, not from my part nor from Rueen's part."

"Tell me your story then…"

"Rueen and I walked in the forest one day, as we had done many times before. Then I heard their little cries and yelps. At first, I did not see them, only their dead mother. It took a while for me to locate their whereabouts. Five little ones. My heart melted, and I quickly realized that these adorable baby fox' would never make it in the harsh environment of the forest. Rueen caught up with me as I had lifted the first baby pups. She looked me in the eyes before she looked at the pup. Then she realized, as I had, that these pups would not make without our help. She took the first pup from my arms, and as she did, I lifted the next. She did something with the first, and then let it go. As she did, it had changed in posture and attitude. More confident as if it had a goal and a place in this world. The others still had their helplessness and were still terrified and anxious. She took the second from me, and I lifted the third. As I held the third, I could feel its shiver, but it seemed to trust me and gave me a quick lick on my nose. As Rueen let the second one go, it showed the same transformation. I handed her all the pups, one by one, and they all ran off. I never thought of them again, but in the moment, I felt a great deal for them."

"Interesting. It seems, even if you are not aware and you do not plan it, your choices accidently lead to larger consequences. I wonder what it is about you that makes it so."

"It has to be, because it was nothing more to it…"

For once, everything that Roy said was true, nothing was added, exaggerated or left out. But the wizard was also right, Rueen had left the pups to their crude destiny. But out of her affection to Roy she intervened in the cause of nature without knowing the consequences of it. And normally, the consequences were something she and Groll often discussed before doing something.

"Still interesting with the choices you make, and why you make them…"

"I've been thinking. Groll and Rueen. Their power, life essence and the two moons. There is a connection, isn't there?

Dialog IV

"Very observant of you, and yes, there is."

"What I have not been able to figure out is what the link is, but I know they are connected somehow."

"Indeed, they are."

"So, are you going to tell me about it or is it something I am not supposed to know?"

"Well no, it is actually a rather small thing, but still a thing I am very proud of to have designed."

"Designed? How do you mean?"

"You have met the creators, they are rather small. And yet they need an infinite supply of life essence in order to be able to fulfil their tasks as creators. Not an easy equation to crack. So, I created a link between the moons and the creators, harvesting the energy of the sun, concentrating it through the heart of the creators and releasing it as life essence inside of them."

"So, the red moons were there from the start?"

"Well, not from the start, but from before I created the creators."

"And the link from the moons to their heart?"

"Advanced stuff, something about quantum physics that you will not understand, but let's just say that it is a kind of invisible road that goes directly from the entire moon structure to the centre of the beating heart in each creator. And as the moon harvests the energy from the sun's beams, it transfers it to the heart of the creator, and it is in the heart of the creator that it is being processed to life essence."

"A link you say? And when the hearts stop beating, the link is severed, and then the moon turns red?"

"Well, yes, in a way. Before this link, the moons were blue. And as I established the link, the draining of sun energy from the moons themselves made them change colour. The same is true from when the link is severed. Only now the moons are redesigned to harvest energy and they are filling up with energy. So, I expect the colours of the moons to change over time, but red for now."

"I have seen the two blue moons once, a long time ago, literally it seems."

"Yes, I believe you have already experienced some time jumps to different periods in this world's linear timeline…"

"Linear timeline? Anyway, a new thought. The red moons that will rise tonight. The one that used to be attached to Rueen, and the one that will be severed from Groll soon. Do they have the same shade of red or will it differ since Rueen have been severed for a very long time?"

"I expect them to have different shades of red, but that is something we will find out tonight!"

"Can they be reattached to someone new?"

"Can they what?"

"Can the moons be linked to new creators, or new individuals that will get the life essence instead of Rueen and Groll?"

"Now you are doing it again Roy!"

"Doing what?"

"Having heavy impact on the linear future of this world. And on its linear past."

"What do you mean?"

"The less you know my friend…"

"Ok… I only got the idea from an episode in one of the many wars I have seen…"

"Please do tell me, dear Roy!"

Turning the flow according to Roy

"This was during a battle by the sea. The cold bloods had attacked one of the fortresses of the warm bloods for a little over a week. The warm bloods were losing ground and were in desperate need of reinforcement. None were scheduled to arrive shortly, and giving the state of the war, none was expected at all. It was desperate times. The cold bloods on the other hand seemed to be gaining strength for each attacking wave, and growing in numbers, even if they kept losing men on the battlefield every day. I fought for the warm bloods at the time. Really stupid war if you ask me. Anyhow, one of the commanding officers had a nervous breakdown and the remainder of his squad, including me, were waiting for our next orders. None came, so we continued doing what we had been doing the past days: using what we could find around us to try and keep the enemy from storming our stronghold that slowly fell apart, piece by piece. The fortress was built in layers, barriers that would protect us into the heart of it. The most outer shell had already collapsed, and a former tower from it had fallen into the river that ran on one side of it. The river heavily protested at the presence of the former tower and tried to push it out of the way, but the tower structure was solid and did not bend to the rivers will. As we waited for our orders and did as best we could, we started to talk about if we could use the river to our advantage somehow. From one side we were protected by a steep mountainside. On a second side was thick forest. And on the third side it was the river, which meant that all attacks either could come from the front in great force from the open field, with difficulty from the forest side or from too far a distance on the opposite shore of the river. The more we looked at the tower in the river, the more we felt that we could use this to our advantage. After a long day's constant attacks from the field side, we hoped that the enemies retaliated for the day and prayed that they would not continue their attacks at night. We were all exhausted. Even so, we somehow found courage and strength to undertake a risky mission. The remainder of our squad left the fortress in hiding and started to carry and drag any and all lumber we could move starting to clog the river and by doing so, redirect the waterflow to flood the field in front of our fortress. Our escapade took the better part of the night and right before the dawn we were not able to move a single straw to add to our pile. It had become more and more difficult to get close enough to the blockade to add anything more. And as the first raindrops started to fall, we crawled back into the fortress again, seeking its protection once more. The rain that day was really heavy, and it was lucky for us for two reasons. The first being the effect it had on our enemies, they had very little shelter and was heavily affected by the rain. The second, and most important. As the heavy rain reached the river all the way upstream, it dragged loose mud, dirt and other small things with the stream. All this helped in clogging the blockade even more. Already by noon the field in front of our fortress was waterfilled, both from the rain and the redirected river. And by the next day it was almost impossible for the cold bloods to attack even if they bravely tried, over and over again."

Turning the flow in reality

There was an awful war, one of far too many, and Roy participated in it as a soldier on the side of the warm bloods. But his cowardness did only server himself to keep him out of harms ways. And as the other surviving members of his squad snuck out that night to clog the river, Roy remained behind, too scared to leave the fortress. In a way, that single decision saved all of them, so in all fairness he is a hero. But the only reason for this is that if he had joined the others, there would have been more people for the enemy scouts to spot. And they would have spotted their initiative if they had organized themselves a little different, as they would have if Roy joined them. Then they all would have been killed, and the fortress would have been invaded the next day. But since Roy did not dare to join them, they had to make do with much less resources and organized themselves to make smaller changes and take smaller objects, leaving the bigger ones behind. And that made all the difference. The enemy scouts did not detect their movements, nor the changes in the debris surrounding the fortress.

And the part where Roy is a hero, even a coward, a thief and a liar can be a hero. But most people's prejudice stops other people from developing and changing. In order to allow other people to change, you have to keep an open mind and be supportive and not judge them when they fail or fall back into old behaviours. The most common reason that stops people from changing is the expectations and treatment by others.

You will see more of Roy's changes over time, if you keep an open mind and let him change. Just like you have changed over time. Maybe you have experienced just that, a person in your surrounding that does not expect you to change or accepts the changes you have gone through and treats you the same, throughout time? Don't do this to Roy, let him change, have patience with him, it will pay off. Granted, he is a slow learner and as a person, he often retaliates to familiar ground once in a pressured situation. But don't we all from time to time?

Dialog V

"Sounds like an amazing story. What made you think of this now?"

"You said that the energy from the moons flowed down to Groll's and Rueen's hearts. I figured if it flows anything that is close to how a river floats, then it must be able to redirect somehow."

"And right you are, even if I have never thought of that possibility."

"Then the harvested energy of the moons does not go to waste, I like that!"

"So, do I, my friend, so do I."

"But does it also mean that there will be two new creators?"

"Two, or one, depending on how the reconnection and redirection is made."

"So, you could direct all the energy to a single individual who would get a lot of energy, or to two individuals, who would get an equal amount of energy?"

"Yes, and no. See, the system was originally designed for one individual, but the first individual that got the total amount of energy could not stand its great powers. It was also a troll, that is why I divided it into two receivers, a companionship."

"So, a physically bigger individual could probably withstand the energy from both moons."

"Well, it's not always about size you know."

"Ok, but in theory it would be possible to reinforce one person with all the life essence instead of two persons?"

"Yes, but my guess is that it ruins the balance. Which is the utter most important thing we all need to obey. That is probably why it did not work the first time!"

"Balance? Like in not falling?"

"No, more like holding a plate with a sphere on it. The plate has no edges, and you are only allowed to hold it with one hand beneath the plate and hold it over your head while you need to walk between one point an another on a specified, unknown time. Should the sphere fall off the plate at any point, your entire life will be over, and life, as we know it, will end. Should you not walk fast enough your entire life will be over, and all life, as we know it, will end. Should you walk too fast and still manage to keep the sphere on the plate and your entire life will be over, and life, as we know it, will end."

"Sounds a lot like not falling to me…"

"Yes, falling would be a bad thing, but if you would fall without dropping the sphere and still managed to walk the distance on time it would not matter that you had fallen."

"I see, but it still sounds like a hard task to complete."

"Yes, that is how it is, the balance in nature is fragile. And we need to do our best to help nature to keep the balance, in every single detail. Should we disrupt the balance, even a little bit. It has devastating consequences."

"It reminds me of another story…"

"Do share, dear Roy."

The impressive balance act at the fair according to Roy

"Once when I was at a market fair, I had just had me a fine glass of Gizzy, first in many years, and it was as tasteful as I remembered it. The table I was sitting by had a view over the town plaza and at the centre of it, amongst all the tables of various goods, from fragile pottery to spices and other eatable things, a loud man started to proclaim that everything in life came down to balance."

"A wise man, I assume?"

"Maybe, but after a while of loud proclamation he pulled out a long stick, twice his own length. It looked as if it materialised out of thin air. All of a sudden in his hand, like it had been there the whole time, but no one saw it there from the beginning. And just like that, he placed the stick on the ground and climbed it, standing on its top on one foot, still rambling about the importance of balance in life."

"Impressive skill, standing on one foot on top of a long stick!"

"Yeah, and that is not half of it. Those with the table closest around him moved their tables, scared that he might fall and land on their tables, damaging their goods. But he did not fall. Instead, he took out another long stick, out of thin air, equally long as the other. He placed it beneath the foot he balanced on, and out of nowhere, he pulled out a mountain goat that he threw out on the far end of the stick while he himself moved to the other end of the stick, creating a T-shaped stick-structure with a goat on one side and a rambling man on the other. Then another stick that he placed on his end of the T and climbed up to the higher level, while throwing down a hen on the back of the goat, to keep the balance of the T-structure."

"Three long sticks, a goat and a hen, out of thin air, that itself sounds like an astonishing performance…"

"Indeed, and a top of it all, he took out a flute and started to play and sing on top of the unlikely structure of sticks animals and the singing mad man. Did not take long for the town law arrested him and threw him out of the town. Which in a way reminded me of the first day I saw you for the first time!"

"Even though it had not happened yet, in the timeline of this world."

"Exactly, and it gave me an idea at the time, but it took me years to finalize it.

"What was that idea?"

"How I would finance the entire sky road."

"And how would that be done?"

"By using my knowledge of the future to benefit in the current present where I found myself at that time."

The impressive balance act at the fair in reality

This story was in fact all true, but he left out a few details. Or rather, not a few, a lot of details. And to start a while before the Gizzy, Roy came to the town and really desperately wanted Gizzy. So, his first mission was to get money to buy it. In order to do this, he stole a pelt from a poorly loaded wagon. With this single piece of peltry he swindled some traders by saying he had a whole cart full of pelts just like it, at least 25, but probably more than 30, and he wanted badly to return home, so if they could agree to pay for 20 pelts and pay upfront he would return shortly with the cart to deliver the goods. For some unknown reason they did pay up front and let Roy go to get their new cargo, but of course, he never returned but got away with a considerable amount of money. From previous experience, he knew his time was limited at the fair with a scam of that magnitude, so he hurried to the nearest place with Gizzy and ordered a glass. The first glass was oh so tasteful. And the second. And the third. And the fourth. By now, he felt the Gizzy warming up his inside, numbing his senses and slowing down his reactions. The fifth was the one that sealed this part of his faith. The swindled traders had found him. Of course, furious. As they dragged him out of the cantina and searched his pockets for the remainder of their money, they covered him with kicks and punches. As Roy lay there, he saw the performance of the extraordinary man on the sticks. And while everything else faded away he focused on what the man was doing and saying. Balance. Then he realized that he had a possibility to change everything. He could use his knowledge of the future to become rich. Gather all the resources necessary to build and sustain the sky road. He could use the balance of his life and of time itself to affect the bigger balance.

As he lay there in the middle of the kicks and punches and studied the man's performance, he suddenly became aware of the man's face. Not that he had seen his own reflexion that many times, but that man looked a lot like himself. And when he looked back at this event, he was uncertain if it was true, or if it was either his mind, memory or the Gizzy that played a game with him.

Swindling the dwarves according to Roy

"How did you build your fortune then?"

"The first thing I thought of was the dwarves and what Phidas said on the sky road when he explained the basics of dwarf economics to Oaks. So, I tried to remember what gemstones and ores or metals that were expensive in my youth. And then, without meeting the dwarves in person, with trading decoys as middle hands, I signed trade agreements with the dwarves. At first it was hard, and I did not make much money of it, but after a while I got the hang of it."

"How did you use your basic knowledge in dwarf economics?"

"You see, at the time, there was a shortage of a red gemstone, Ruby. And it was very expensive. I But I remembered that in my youth, Ruby was rather common, even amongst man. So, I knew that it would fall in price. And since the dwarf model of trading with humans was once each summer, it was not hard to get a deal with one of the dwarf traders to sign up for buying Ruby from me, a rather big trade, and pay me in gold. You see, gold has always been expensive throughout time. I designed the deal one summer, only to get it delivered two summers from that point in time. The agreement was simple. Two barrels of Ruby against a crate of gold. As we struck the deal, the dwarf party was very pleased with himself and I was told that my business tactics was rather stupid. But during those two summers, Rubies became pretty common and the price dropped like a stone in the ocean. For one small gold coin I could get two barrels of Rubies that summer. For me it was a great deal, and for the dwarf, not so much. But, from what I heard later he gained in status directly after making the deal, and because of that he became quite wealthy, so I guess we were both sitting on a winning hand at the end of the day."

"No harm done then, even if you could say that you tricked the dwarf."

"No harm done that would be my motto. And yes, you could say that I swindled the dwarf, but in my defence, it was a risky business for me as well."

"Risky how?"

"I could not say for certain when I made the deal, but I believed that it would take about two summers before the price dropped. But it could be five as well, or twelve, no way of telling which. And if the price had not dropped, I would be in a lot of trouble."

"And if that would be the case, it wouldn't be the first time you were in trouble?"

"Not at all, some say, or rather said, that trouble is my middle name."

"I would be one of them…" the wizard laughed, and so did Roy.

"I guess I would be too…"

Both kept laughing for a while, and then Roy continued.

"…that crate with gold was my cornerstone to building the rest of the fortune."

"And you managed to invest it wisely to earn more?"

"No, not really, but my investments payed off… in large parts due to more speculative business with the dwarves."

"I see…"

Swindling the dwarves in reality

Roy was rather truthfully in that story, but as most of the times when Roy tells the truth, there are things he is leaving out that would clutter the pureness of his story.

In this case, when he made the deal through a trading decoy, he had just lost all his earnings from a period of hard work with stealing and plundering. The lowlifes called him 'The Hood' since he always covered himself with the hood on his shirt when engaged in a robbery or he plundered a transport or something of that sort.

His reputation was fears and those who joined his franchise where at best questionable in their own agendas. Most joined him only for one or two heists, and then dared not to continue working with him, because he always disagreed with each and every member of his crew. This was a carefully worked out strategy from Roy's part, and he himself had built up the reputation in advance, just to make it easier to succeed with ever transaction (as he preferred to call it).

He had even succeeded in terrifying the local law in the area where he operated, so he had little or no intervention when the transactions took place, and afterward there were usually little questions when the stolen objects, treasures or money showed up in circulation, it was simply accepted and often considered lucky for those who had lost them in the first place, since they now could purchase their items back, often at a very low price, way below market price.

The problem for Roy was that he was never a businessman, and always lived day by day, from hand to mouth. And when he engaged in trading with the dwarves, it was the first time he actually thought of the future and how he could secure the funds to build the sky road.

As a man with a lot of time on his hands, Roy took his new mission with great patience, and perhaps for the first time in his life, he had a goal and enjoyed working towards it. In the beginning with very little luck and a lot of setbacks, but as time passed his trading skills was sharpened and his eye for running a large enterprise developed to truly unmatchable.

Swindling the dwarves was a first step and was kind of a crossroad were Roy left his old path and turned to a new.

The attempt on the dwarf crown jewels according to Roy

"One great thing about trading with the dwarves was all the stories they'd share. Each summer, when they came to trade, they always shared new stories."

"Ah, riches come in many forms. Stories can indeed lead to a richer life, which is one of the reasons I joined you here today…"

"Are you up for more stories then?"

"Always, give it your best!"

"One of the dwarf traders told my contact that the dwarf crown jewels were hidden in a secret compartment in the mountain. They had hidden them from the outside to ensure that no dwarf would be able to find it."

"Sounds very unlikely to me, they have always locked away their most valuable things in vaults inside the mountain. Vaults built to withstand all known dwarf mining techniques."

"Huh, I did not know that."

"You live, and you learn, something new every day!"

"Yes, anyway. I was so curious as to see if I could find them, so I went on another trip to the mountain. From my previous experience I could easily believe that they would have an entrance to a compartment that was hidden to the naked eye."

"Truly masters of mountain craft!"

"I looked for the place that the dwarf described and found something that matched his description very well. And I could find a hidden entrance. But I was disappointed. The hidden chamber and all its compartments were empty."

"A decoy, perhaps?"

"Maybe, but I could not find anything there and continued my search elsewhere. And to my surprise, I found another place that was not only a match to the description, but a perfect match."

"Did you find anything?"

"Oh, I found something alright, but not what I was looking for."

"Not the crown jewels?"

"No, something far more interesting. I found a hidden entrance to a cave system. And from that system I found a small tunnel to a great hall. In the middle of the hall was a nest with a silver egg. And should it have been only that, I would have taken it for a dragon egg. But the entire hall was filled with werewolves."

"Werewolves? Did you walk right into the cave were Groll and Rueen had hidden their life essence?"

"Yes, it seemed that way. And the strange thing was that as I entered the cave, all the werewolves seemed to wake up from a deep slumber. At first, I thought they would attack, but they didn't. It took me a while to figure out why."

"Why didn't they attack you then?"

"Because they cannot touch the life essence. And because they cannot, they can't harm anything with a higher amount of life essence than ordinary humans…"

"…and you have a higher amount of life essence than ordinary humans, curtesy of Groll…"

"Exactly, so I could move freely around in the cave, navigating between all the werewolves, completely unharmed. It was only when I came close to the egg that they intervened and physically blocked my way to the egg."

"Their protective instinct…"

"Yes, so no crown jewels, but something far more valuable and interesting."

The attempt on the dwarf crown jewels in reality

Roy were looking for the dwarf crown jewels. But he did not know that it was a made-up story that the dwarf traders told as part of their trading strategy. A customer that had listened to a story tended to be happier and more relaxed, and a little distracted, which made it easier to get a higher price for their goods.

But Roy did not know that and set out to steal them and perhaps sell them back to the dwarves at a later time. And this was his first time he was looking for it, but not the last. It was not until this very day that he realised that the story he had heard was most likely not true. Kind of like his own stories. Even if, in his defence, his stories were mostly based on true events, with extraordinary things added and removed as it fitted.

In a way, he felt tricked, a dream of finding (or rather stealing) the valuable dwarf crown jewels, no longer in reach. A dream built on lies. Lies meant to entertain, to misinform, mislead and distract from the deal that were about to be made.

A brief moment, Roy thought about if his stories had the same effect on other people, fooling them for a while only to later find out that they believed a lie. But like the water runs of a gooses feathers, the thought escaped his mind and took its place among the million other thoughts that evaded his conscious. Thoughts that slowly gathered up and soon would outnumber the stars of the night sky.

Saving the girls from the fire according to Roy

"Did it scare you to find yourself among all the werewolves?"

"Not the least, well, a little in the beginning, but not after I figured out that they would not harm me."

"Would you say you are brave and unafraid?"

"Yes, in a way. If there were any medals given for bravery, I would already have deserved a few."

"Tell my one of those times!"

"There was this one time, I was on my way from the northern parts down south. It was time to start a new life again. Since I don't age like everyone else, I need to restart my life about every tenth or fifteenth summer. I have always chosen summer since it is easier to travel. And I always started south and worked my way up north in about eight to ten-day journeys to minimize the chance of anybody else crossing my path that could recognize me from my 'past lives'."

"Wise strategy, I am impressed!"

"I was passing by a house that were on fire. I had seen the smoke rise to the sky a while, so I had not much hope of finding the house enterable and thus not being able to help if it were needed. But as I arrived, I saw that there was still time to go into the house before the fire consumed it all. And as I entered, I heard cries from what I assumed was children. They were terrified from the sound of their screams. They were hard to locate in the smoke and the tiny pieces of ashes that cluttered the air inside. Had I arrived a few minutes later, it would not have been possible to enter the house, both due to the heat and the visibility inside. But now I managed to locate them and bring them all out. Three scared little girls. The youngest only one summer old."

"Brave indeed! Where were their parents?"

"I never found out. I took the girls to the next house that I could find and told them what had happened. They promised to take care of the girls and investigate what had happened. They knew the family well."

"A deed worthy of a medal of honour, if anyone would give it."

"Yes, but my reward was only to help, and to know that those little girls would be able to live on, even if that terrible incident ruined their lives in a way."

"So very kind-hearted of you."

"I got a place to stay for the night, and food, even food to carry with me on my journey. So I was well awarded at the time."

"I understand. But it must have felt good to make a difference in somebody else's life? In this case at least three lives?"

"Yes, it is a warm feeling to be able to do something good for others. And often all the reward for the good deed is the gratefulness of the one in the receiving end."

"But sometimes it would be nice to be rewarded in any other way?"

"Yes, I suppose…"

"Like being immortal?"

"Huh, I never thought about it like that… but I guess… I received a tremendous gift from Groll that day, err, today I mean… I guess that it is always a question about perspective?"

Saving the girls from the fire in reality

As Roy saw smoke rising in a distance, he figured two things. From the colour of the smoke, it looked like the fire had just started. Secondly, if he hurried, he might get to where the fire was with time to loot the place, if the fire was in a house or barn or any other manmade building.

As he arrived at the scene he figured that it was almost too late, but since it was a house there was a good chance he could find some food or some things of value that he could sell further down the road. It was worth a quick look to see if there was something easy to grab.

He found it strange that the house owners did not stand outside to watch the fire, but he could not believe that there would be people still inside the house, that was a thought that never crossed his mind.

And when he went inside for his own benefits, and heard the cries from the girls, he was taken by surprise and was not sure how to act. He snooped around a little and found a jar with money on a shelf in the kitchen which he emptied down his pocket, some jewellery by a drawer with a little mirror on top. They also found their way down his pocket.

Then it was something inside him that woke up and he could no longer stand the cries from the children, so he went further into the house and found them and just managed to get them out before the raging fire consumed the entire building.

As he stood there, with the three girls, he did not know what to do. He wanted to leave them there and carry on with his own business, but something did not feel right in doing so.

Roy ended up with carrying the little one on one arm, holding the middle one in the other hand and slowly walked down the road in hopes to find someone or somewhere to leave the girls.

What he never knew, and never found out, was that the youngest girl, the one he carried on his arm, was the great grandmother of Yena.

As he arrived at a nearby house, they recognised the children and was terrified to hear about the house and the fire. They promised to take care of the girls and offered Roy shelter and food for the night as gratitude for saving the girls. The things he 'salvaged' from the burning house he kept safe in his own pockets for later use.

Living as an immortal according to Roy

"Tell me, dear Roy, I am curious, how have you coped with going from a mortal being to be almost immortal? What does that do to a person?"

"Oh, heavy question. How am I going to answer that?"

Roy thought for a while and the wizard said nothing, just admired their great view. After a while Roy continued.

"At first, I did not think much about it, probably more because I had to adapt to a new period in time… but as time passed, it became more obvious that my new 'enhancements' made me different. I have always been a loner, more or less, but have still surrounded me with acquaintances that have been able to provide and support me in various aspects of my day-to-day life. I did not age, they did. And it did not grow on me until one of my contacts commented on it. And then it spread like a fire. They accused me of sorcery, and all turned on me. So, I had to make a quick exit."

"An unplanned drastic change in life…"

"Certainly. I had nothing planned, nothing saved up, so I had to start from scratch again. As a beggar. But back then it was no big deal, no vampires, no undead, no werewolves. Only people to take into consideration. And since I was up north at the time, I figured I'd walk far from my present location and travelled all the way south to get a fresh start. And during that long walk I promised myself to never repeat that again. I worked out my strategy of periodically movement, but it took me a few moves before I could manage to find a suitable strategy for making arrangements in advance to ease the transactions."

"I am under the impression that you never changed your name."

"No, not once. Never saw the need for it before. It was only before I decided to come and sit here to avoid meeting my younger self that I realised that it perhaps would have been a good idea to do so."

"Why is that?"

"Well, my name has started to appear in historical contexts here and there. But fortunate for me is that my name is rather common, both first name and sir name. And besides, it is pretty hard to imagine that Roy 'The robbin' Hood' Hicks or the Roy Hicks that are mentioned in the war of the Wizards are the same individual as me. I mean, I am alive now, how could I possibly have lived when those historical events took place?"

"Yes, how could you possibly? No man in his right mind would ever believe that!"

"I know, it was even hard to convince Vladir at first, and then Yena."

"Even Vladir? You'd think that a being that can live forever would be humbler and accept that there could be others that share that faith."

"You would think so, but it was not until he notices that I did not age as the others that he fully believed in me."

"Then again, isn't Vladir known for his stubbornness."

Roy laughed.

"Yes, or at least he was, until he fell in love with Yena that is…"

"Has he changed?"

"No, not really, but compared to Yena, Vladir is not half as stubborn."

"I see… well, stubbornness can be quite useful sometimes. I know that from my own experience."

"You mean from the whole house thing?"

"I mean from that whole house thing for one…"

Living as an immortal in reality

All Roy's acquaintances have always been people that have been doing things for Roy. They have all had in common that they fix things for Roy and fix things for the others surrounding Roy. He has always acted as a man in the middle and have almost never, at least for the first ages of his life, done anything for anybody else than himself. Not a very characteristic thing for who Roy is turning out to be but let us see it as a very long childish phase, that lasted far longer for Roy than for most infants that are completely self-centred.

His strategy did develop over time and he got pretty good at ending a life on one place while preparing for the next in another place. Always without letting his acquaintances figure out what was going on.

The good thing for them in having somebody like Roy in their close proximity is that Roy always got himself well connected. Through Roy, almost anything could be fixed and managed. The price for it was doing stuff for Roy. But to most, it was a fair price to pay, as their benefits almost always was higher than their entry fee.

Roy was good in that perspective, sure, he used others for his own purpose, but he tried to repay them through his other contacts.

As for changing his name, he had never really thought about it, but had started to get comments on that people had heard of another Roy Hicks. And at first, he thought that he had not moved long enough from his previous life and that he was haunted by his own past present. But it always turned out to be in some sort of historic reference. And given Roy's nature, having experienced the past, he never found the historic text any interesting and dismissed most of them as incomplete or fake.

And to be honest, he rarely could take credit for what his historic version had done. Most of the time it was completely bogus, for example the historic reference to his said participation in the Wizard war.

He was in the war, and he supported the cold bloods at the time, and their Wizards united under the blue dragon and its flag. But historic reference claimed that he was a warm-blood hero fighting under the red dragon and its flag. And the entire situation was quite embarrassing and not worth mentioning, from Roy's perspective.

As for meeting Vladir, another immortal (although in a very different way), he never found any good way to break the news to Vladir and just spilled his words over an evening breakfast.

Vladir who were used to Roy's imaginative stories did not give the new revelation much credit, until many years later when Roy's lack of aging could not be dismissed any longer.

The Wizard's house according to the Wizard

"Then it's your turn, tell me about the house…"

"Very well. Where do I begin?"

The wizard though for a moment before he continued.

"You know I do not experience time as you do, nor space. Both space and time are forces I can manipulate and control, and move to and through, but I cannot *not* be dependent on them."

"I am not certain I understand."

"See it like gravity to you. You always have to obey gravity, even if you jump of a cliff to dive in to a lake or the ocean, and you are temporarily mid-air, you still are affected by gravity and no matter how high up you jump from, gravity will always pull you down."

"What about the birds? Are they affected by gravity as well?"

"Yes, always, but they can use other forces of nature to fly. They can catch the air with their wings and use it to move themselves around, just like you are walking on solid ground. Or swimming in the water. And when the birds use their wings, they use that force to overcome the force of gravity. But as soon as they stop catching air with their wings, they will also drop like a stone towards the surface again."

"All fascinating, but a bit hard to understand, back to the house please."

"What I am trying to say is that even I have to operate within the frames of time and space. But I wanted to try an experiment. To see if I could make something exist outside of time and space. And I figured out a way to create the house without it existing in space, I could hide it outside of space. And I also could hide it outside of time. But as I did, things got complicated. The first complication was that if I want to build a house here on the ground you have fixed references as to where all objects are placed in relation to one another. And when I built the house outside of space there are no fixed references and no way of place physical objects in relation to one another. To solve this, I had to relate the objects to themselves. But since space (and time) are constantly changing, so does the objects in the house, which is why I had to remove time as a factor as well. If the objects exist not in space and not in time and are related only to each other it works just fine. But. And there is always a but. In order for me to interact with the house I need to enter it. And to enter it, it needs to interact with space. And to be able to exist in space, it needs to exist in time. That is why I needed a place in time and space to be able to enter it. But if there was only one interaction with time and space, I would not be able to exit it. Therefore there are a lot of points in time where the house appears. And just to make it easier, I chose the same space as well, even if I could let it fluxuate. The second challenge was me moving around inside the house. And that is something I was too eager to do, so I did not take into count what the consequences of me interacting with the house would be. Since I exist in time and space, and the house does not, I need to activate time inside the house, but only when I make changes to it. Like opening a door or window. And for each door I open, time starts to flow as soon as I lay hands on the door handle and only stops again when I shut the door behind me. Since time has affected the house, space is also affected, and all the rooms shift places. So, if I enter a room, and close the door behind me, I will not end up in the same room that I just left if I pass through the same door again."

"Sounds very difficult to manoeuvre."

"Indeed. And to get out of the house I needed to be in the entrance the exact same time as the house appears in space and time here. If not, I will not be able to exit the house that time and will have to wait until next time it reappears in time and space."

"And it is because of the whole hidden in time and space thing that there are time ripples here, and it is because of the time ripples I can

81

move through time… so, you are the cause for me being, what did you call it, a 'time wanderer'?"

"Something like that."

The Wizard's house in reality

The Wizard was one of four Wizards. They all played different parts in the multiverse. Our Wizard was indeed the original cause of the time ripples, for which he has accepted full responsibility, even if it was an unfortunate consequence that he did not foresee. And the time ripples did not only affect this world, no, they spread throughout all the multiverses and throughout time. The effect was the strongest here in the centre of it all, but what he did not know was during the time he was caught in his little experimental house, two of the other Wizards visited the place trying to undo the damage caused in the first place. But let us just settle for that they did not make things better. And once they realized this, far too late that is, they stopped their attempts immediately and never spoke of it again. In fact, they pretended that it never had happened. What they did not know was that when the two of them gathered up at ground zero, the fourth Wizard simultaneously from another part in the multiverse tried to counteract the damage in time and space. So, in all, they were all responsible for the current situation, even if only one initiated everything by his hypothetical and experimental house. And the house itself had only one purpose, to satisfy the Wizard's curiosity.

Sadly, the Wizard was not the only one who got trapped in the house, but he was the only one who ever got out of it.

The Wizard tried twice to dismantle it. Once he tried to destroy it, but he only caused more and deeper time ripples. And another time he tried to undo it before it was created, which oddly enough gave him the idea to create it in the first place.

The lesson in this, if there is such a thing in the story of the house, hidden in time and space, is that you should not experiment with things that are outside of reach and perception. Once you cross the border of your own nature, knowledge and wisdom, you cross the line to the unknown. And manoeuvring in the unknown is a very difficult thing and can have devastating consequences. And the paradox in this is that in order to grow in knowledge and wisdom, you need to explore beyond your own border. But let's just recommend that you stay within your own natural borders and at least never cross over that line, no matter how faint it may be.

The Wizard war according to Roy

"You fought in the wizard war?"

"Yes, for the cold-blooded."

"You know there are no such thing as the warm-blooded and the cold-blooded, right?"

"Yeah, I know, Groll taught me that. We are all the same. But it's the common language, and I am so used to that, so I never bother to educate anybody."

"Ever thought perhaps you should?"

"Anyways, I was fighting for the cold-bloods under the flag of the blue dragon. Not that I ever saw the blue dragon, but we were attacked by the red dragon once."

"Really? Attacked by a dragon?"

"Yes, it was said that the warm-bloods had a better dragon tamer than the cold-bloods. But the cold-bloods had an advantage on the wizard tactics and battle plan."

"But still, attacked by a dragon? Sounds highly unlikely…"

"It nearly bit my head off!"

"That's a story I'd like to hear!"

"We were on the front, and we spread out in the treetops, trying to be both invisible and preparing for an ambush. At the time I was quite used to being in a treetop, because I had done a great deal of preparations and studies to prepare for the work with the sky road, so I felt a little like coming home as soon as we climbed those trees."

"Must have been a sight, men climbing treetops like monkeys!"

"Perhaps, but I did not feel like a monkey. At least not until the dragon attacked. Then we were rather sitting ducks than monkeys. Easy prey for a huge, hungry dragon. It landed in the middle of our trees, about four treetops from me. And it was furious. Instantly attacked with fire. She had her back against me at first, so the flames torched three nearest treetops, counting away from her."

"Did anyone attack her? Sounds like she got aggressive…"

"Are you some kind of dragon expert? I have no idea if she were under the spell of the dragon trainer or what, but she attacked unprovoked. We all were 'crap-in-our-pants-scared' as soon as we saw her silhouette in the sky. A dragon was not really the opponent we sought out to fight…"

"I am sorry, I was not meaning to interfere with your story, continue please."

"Thank you, and as I were saying, she attacked without provocation. The first three members in my group were, we hope, incinerated directly. We barely heard their screams through the roar of the dragon and the horrible sound of the burning trees. She turned towards me, and the first three trees suffered the same faith as the previous three. Leaving me with three burning trees, a dragon and another three burning trees. As I was about to descend from the tree, out of nowhere came a battalion of warm bloods. Luckily, all of us saw them, and neither descended. If just one of us had we'd all been compromised, and I would probably not be here today, immortal or not. The newcomers had no idea we were there and focused all their energy on the dragon, trying to get her airborne again. I am not certain, but I think she took some of them with her, as she arose from the ground and sprung up in the air like an arrow, only after she had opened her great, wide jaws aiming them in my direction. But she missed me, took a big bite out of the closest tree instead. The battalion rapidly cleared the perimeter, luckily for me since the fire had started to spread to my treetop by now. We had no other choice but to retreat and regroup. I am certain that she sentenced us and choose to attack us, and should her allies have noticed us, they would probably had ordered her to obliviate us."

The Wizard war in reality

Roy was proud to have given the idea to plan the ambush from the treetops. And as they prepared the ambush on the warm-bloods and infiltrated the treeline at the front, where they expected the warm-bloods to pass, the red dragon really landed in the middle of them all.

They could not see that she had a wound at one of her legs and her rage were only connected to the pain she was feeling. Dragons are not hostile, as you'd think, nor are they feeding on anything they see moving, as is commonly believed.

Those that hurried to her upon her landing was her care team. They only wanted to tend for her wounds. And as she flew off again, they hurried after to hopefully be able to tend her at her next landing site.

The truth is that the dragon did *discover the men in the trees. But only after have setting half a dozen trees on fire. By leaving the site, she tried to protect the others hiding in the treetops. Dragons are intelligent. She understood that it was enemy forces and by leading 'her own side' away from them she could hopefully spare lives on both sides.*

Just before she flew away, she saw that a branch on fire were about to fall over and light the tree Roy sat in. Of course, it was inevitable that it would eventually catch on fire, but she still bit of the branch delaying the fire a while, to try and buy time for the poor soul that were stuck in the tree.

Rather a hero than a fears monster, but misunderstood by the great part of the population, hunted by the dwarves, 'tamed' by man (which is rather a mixture of brainwashing and various spells). And the sad thing is that it was only one wizard that performed this on all dragons. In a way supporting both sides of the conflict. But that was a well-kept secret known only by the wizard. A wizard with a plan.

Sky road construction according to Roy

"That was a story alright. I know dragons, and I find it hard to believe, but you were there, so I will not argue over it…"

"Having your head almost chewed off by a dragon is not something that one easily forgets…"

"I completely understand that. But you reminded me about the construction of the sky road. Do tell me more."

"Alright. Sky road. What do you want to know?"

"Well, first of all, I have a good idea on how you funded it. But how did you convince people working on it, and working with a vampire? How did you meet him anyway? And perhaps the most important, the undead. Why do you want to control their movement?"

"Hold your horses, one thing at the time. First, constructing the sky road and convincing people to work with a vampire. As for working with a vampire, I never told people about it, and said we had to work at night to avoid being seen. Which also were true. Vladir himself wanted to be the one who revealed to the group at a later time, after they had gotten to know him. This of course only worked with the first group that boarded the work. Then it spread by rumour, which almost made him a legend to all newcomers. That benefited our work, so we never tried to change anything after that. And as for constructing the sky road. At first, money was the single motivator in getting people to work on it. But as our secret building project started to spread, we got a new type of workers that genuinely believed in our objectives. And once that culture was founded, things worked much smoother."

"And what was, or rather is, your objectives?"

"In its foundation the sky road is a liberation tool. When the time comes, and I believe it is very close. The sky road will be used to move hordes of undead to meet up the coming rise of the vampire army, that I myself have set in motion, and hopefully reducing the harm done to the dwarf army and the armies of the warm-bloods and cold-bloods that have also been gathered for new fights. And there is a rumour of a sixth army, that I cannot make heads or tails of. It seems to either arise from the ocean or from slavers and other merchants from the north."

"So, your liberation is to neutralize both the vampire army and the hordes of the undead to let the other armies fight amongst themselves?"

"It sounds harsh when you say it like that, but in all fairness, the dwarf army is only interested in fighting amongst their own kin. The warm-bloods and the cold-bloods have a long history of fighting and as for the sixth army I am puzzled. But my point being that if we by using the sky road can move up the undead to meet up with the vampire army, then all the other four can mind their own business with at least two opponents lesser to worry about. If we do not move the undead or fail in our attempt to get the undead and the vampires to clash, I assume that all the others will have to fight more battles with greater loss on all sides."

"Then why provoke the vampires in the first place?"

"I think we all agree that it is enough with the life in this world that sprung from the hands for Rueen and Groll. The man-made life is not something that benefits this world and if we can, with or without the sky road, in any way liberate this world from all the suffering they cause."

"Aren't you forgetting one 'army'?"

"What do you mean?"

"I mean the sole offspring of Rueen and Groll that were created in a narrow single purpose."

"Ah, yes, I have left them out of the equation."

"Why?"

"I am counting with that the death of Groll somehow also will mean the death of the werewolves."

"Ah, but what if I tell you that you are wrong?"

"Then the liberation movement of the sky road have another task to complete."

"And if the liberation movement would count as one army and the werewolves as another, then it would be eight forces in movement right now?"

"Yes, sounds about right."

"Then I can reveal that your fifth army in reality are two different armies."

"Then it would be nine forces in the play."

"And ten if you count the rouge wizard. She is a party not to forget in this equation!"

"Rouge wizard?"

"Ah, yes, she left the party just before you and Phidas arrived. In fact, she is the reason Groll died."

Sky road construction in reality

Again, most of the things Roy said about the sky road and the way it was constructed is true. Also, the part where it became living legend and attracted those who believed in its idea. The difference this time was that Roy did not leave anything out or added something to make the story more interesting.

The only thing worth mentioning is perhaps that as Roy set out to build the sky road, he knew it was going to be used for moving hordes of undead. What he did not know was why *they needed to move the hordes of the undead. That is something that took years for Roy to figure out, and he did not really start to think about it until the construction of the sky road started.*

At first, he did not share many thoughts regarding the philosophy behind it all, with the exception of Vladir, and eventually Yena. But by the time Yena was part of their team the overall strategies were all out in the open.

And overall, the big challenges were to keep a huge construction project like this a secret. Roy approached this to officially keep the profile of a rich mad man that just had to make his surreal construction project happened. Well aware that this approach would make the whole enterprise more expensive. But at the time for staring the construction money was not one of Roy's issues in life and after the construction start, he went back to use trading decoys once again.

Any modern corporate leader would be wise to spend time with Roy and try to get him to reveal his trading secrets, businessman ship and to try to replicate his incredible logistic skills. But now-a-days Roy is not into business anymore, and should any modern corporate leader find Roy and actually take time to talk to him, he would very successfully deceive them to buy his current presentable constructed veneer and very quickly leave him be.

Meeting Vladir according to Roy

"Sounds like we are in a little over our head. Ten different armies that may collide at any time, including one rouge wizard that killed Groll."

"Indeed, I figured it is best you know. I have a feeling you might find this information valuable to get out of any tough situations that may soon come down the road."

"Speaking of which, tough situations, that is how I met Vladir."

"Do tell."

"At the time I was pursuing the possibility to buy the vampire stronghold and blow it up before they moved in. But I was too late. When I approached it, I ran into a vampire guard that took me prisoner. So, happened to be that Vladir was working on some door to their masters living quarters. Or main hall, which was the same thing. He carved events from the vampire timeline. The guard that had imprisoned me was inside talking to the master, and I got time alone with Vladir."

"But at the time you did not know him, and he did not know you?"

"No, but I briefly knew him from my first encounter with him along with Phidas and had understood that he hosted hostility towards what the vampire master drove the vampire clan to be. So, I said that to him, without explaining how I knew it. And I said that he could have a great life outside of the castle. Perhaps not an easy one, but a free life. And that I needed his help not to end up as vampire dinner. Time was running short any I knew that he could not do much, but perhaps something. I later found out that I had touched all the right buttons inside him and that he started to execute a plan to escape the castle. But now modified his plan to free me in the process."

"Had he that much influence at the vampire master?"

"No, not at all, so he bullshitted up a story and said that he needed my blood memories since I had seen so much beauty in the world. Beauty he needed to take part of as inspiration for his ongoing work at the castle."

"Did the master buy it?"

"Yes, but probably only because he had fed recently and was pleased with the work Vladir did for him. Vladir got me as a little extra payment and a token of appreciation."

"And then he could escape with you?"

"No, it took many summers more until he could escape, but he freed me, let me out at dawn. But only after tasting my blood."

"How did he taste your blood?"

"He bit me, I still got the scars. He needed to do it, he needed my blood-memories or else the whole scam would have been revealed."

"So, he got all your memories. Even the once from before you jumped back in time."

"Yes, he saw himself, the sky road, Yena, and everything else that I had experienced."

"Difficult to hide from the master later?"

"I imagine, we've never talked about it, but I assume it was hard not to reveal anything. Even if it was before the master could actually read and control minds, he still a scary good judgement of character and could read others with a great accuracy."

"Remind me to talk to Vladir about this sometime, will you?"

"Does this mean I will see more of you after today?"

"It does."

"And that Vladir or I will not die anytime soon in the coming fights we might be engaged in?"

"I did not say that. But I see how you can interpret that from what I said."

Meeting Vladir in reality

At first Vladir were unsure if the mad human in front of him actually told the truth. He seemed to do, but he said things he could not possibly know. Things Vladir never told anyone, and it had to be completely made up but true by coincidence.

Vladir asked his master for the human to feed on only to satisfy his curiosity on how he knew the things he claimed to know. He had no intention of sparing Roy at all. After all, humans were only food. And yes, at the time Vladir had forgotten that he once was human, he had suppressed everything from his past human life and did not look back. Even if he did not agree with the master and how he had led the vampire clan up until this point, he still did not see how humans would ever be anything else than food for him.

By blood-memory from Roy he saw a great many things, even the future. He fully understood the danger in this knowledge and even if he did not understand the reason for the current actions, helping Roy escape, he understood the importance of it.

He also saw a bright future for himself, Yena, friendship, commitment to something greater than himself that he could share with others. All things he deeply desired and all were currently out of reach.

This day, Vladir's secret rebellion towards the vampire master started. And it took a few summers to understand and plan, all the time in careful hiding from the master himself.

But all things considered, it seemed like he would pull it off and would be able to enjoy the bright future and the fruits of any hard work he would be able to engage in now.

That was the leading star for Vladir and remained his leading star throughout the ages.

The first step to climb on the ladder was to break free of the vampire clan. Not something that he could easily imagine how to pull off. And the second step was surviving outside of the castle, and the third probably being finding Roy again. But all this only after he successfully had helped Roy escape his current imprisonment.

Letting everybody know that they would meet a different Roy according to Roy

"I will interpret what you just said in my advance and will continue to believe that both I and Vladir will be around for a long time coming."

"I will not comment on that. I believe I have already spilled to much information regarding the future… speaking of which. How did you handle that with your present self and all the people on and around the sky road?"

"My present self? Oh, you mean the me that will jump back through time little later today?"

"Exactly!"

"Well, for most people it was hard to believe, but I stressed out the fact that one day I will leave the sky road. And when I return, it will be me, but not the same me. And that it is absolute prohibited to discuss anything at all regarding me or my role in the sky road. They should all respect that this new Roy would have no knowledge of anything that we had all been through and that they all needed to treat him as a complete stranger, no matter how hard it would be."

"Was it difficult for them to understand it and act accordingly?"

"Well, I did a few practises runs. And left only to return a time afterwards. My first run was a terrible disaster, and it was good that I decided to try it out before the real deal would take place. It took quite a lot of explaining to do, and I had to explain my fear of intervening with the timeline and affect the other me to make different choices that would strand us all in a difficult situation and perhaps a completely different future than we currently live in. This was of course something I do not know, but something that I find most likely."

"And right you are, dear friend. Good thing to do practice runs before the real event took place. I have been watching and I can reassure you that all have played their part exemplary!"

"Feels good to hear. I have been worried. And at the same time, I figure if anything would have gone sour, I would not meet the expected situation this afternoon. But now I can stop being nervous about that."

"Indeed you can, dear Roy. You will be able to pick up the situation right where you left it a long time ago, or if you will, in just a little while."

"It feels strange to view it like that, but also, very logical. You would think that I've had a lot of time adapting to this and get used to the idea, but it still puzzles me a great deal and I have to focus real hard to keep it in mind and make it logical."

"I can imagine the conflicting natures of both thoughts at the same time. But both are true, and not only from one perspective, but from both perspectives. It's often like this with paradoxes. If you stand on one particular place and can find more than one truth, you can often find the same, and sometime plenty more truths from another place. And given the different points of view, the truths in one point does not contradict each other even if they normally would, nor will they contradict any other truth from other points of view."

"Now it's another one of those times where I will pretend that I understood what you just said just so we can move along in our conversation…"

"I am sorry, it's just that I feel the need to explain myself very often."

"No worries, just don't expect your counterpart to understand everything you say, especially if it is a mere human, and not one of your Wizard pals."

"Oh, me and my 'Wizard pals' rarely meet, and even if we do, it is even more rare that we actually talk."

Letting everybody know that they would meet a different Roy in reality

Roy was very confused and nervous and did not know at all how he would communicate this to the others. He knew he had to but had not the faintest idea on how to do it. And at the same time, he was so convinced that it needed to be done and that no one could reveal anything to the 'new Roy' as he referred to himself to the others.

Since he often had practiced strange jokes on the others, they naturally figured that this was yet another and did not take him very seriously. And from that perspective it was good that he did a few practices runs where claimed to leave only to return and pretend to be the 'new Roy'. And the last piece of the puzzle was when he realized that the only way to convince the others was by revealing that when the 'new Roy' arrived, he would do so in company by a dwarf. And not just any dwarf, but Grand Master Phidas himself.

This was something the others could relate to, since they knew that Roy did not know the Grand Master and that it was very unlikely in itself that the Grand Master would show up on the surface. But Roy reassured them that this is what would happen, and that they simply had to trust him on the fact that they could not reveal anything to the 'new Roy' or to Phidas.

This was also the deal breaker that made the whole thing work. When the 'new Roy' and Phidas actually did show up, the others were convinced that it was not their old Roy and Phidas acted as a constant reminder to treat him as a stranger but welcome them at the same time. A hard balance for everybody, but they pulled it off with flying colours and their old Roy would be very proud of them as he returned to the sky road, or rather, what was left of the sky road.

Perhaps this was the first time that Roy actually worried about something this deep, as he was actually scared of the consequences of messing with the timeline, at least when it was something that could possibly affect himself.

Controlling the undead according to Roy

"I'll see if I can answer more of your questions now, I feel like I am a little behind. What have I not covered?"

"I have lost track, but how about a short background on the whole moving the undead around?"

"Yes, I can do that. And I assume you are all familiar with the undead, and that I do not have to explain their nature to you?"

"I know of their nature, but I have never figured out why they were created, or rather, why they were allowed to stay alive, ehr, I mean, undead when they lack the life essence."

"That is a question I have asked myself several times as well. And I cannot find any good answer to it either."

"Yes, but back to moving the hordes around."

"Ah, yes. When we started to build the sky road, I knew that it was used to move hordes of the undead. But I did not really know why or how. And I had never seen it done. But it did not take long time from when we started to build that we encountered a small horde of undead. And we needed to get them moved since they blocked our tools and a lot of material that we were using at the time. What we had was a platform where we could seek refuge. And what we also had was a bunch of ropes that we had tied in nearby trees to use in the construction."

"Sounds like a nice place to wait out the undead."

"It was, a safe haven you might call it. But our problem was that they did not move and after a day stuck at the platform we needed to get going and needed to take some kind of action. One of the lads, Jameson, that were with us in the construction phase said he had an idea that he wished to try. And with those words he took an axe, cut one of the ropes loose and held it in his hand, walked towards the edge of the platform and jumped. Naturally we all grasped of chock, it happened too fast for us to understand and figure out what he did. One second, he rose and mumbled something and the next he jumped. Of course, we all threw ourselves towards the edge to see what happened."

"Well spit it out, what happened?"

"Jameson held tight in the rope and swung it like the most natural thing in the world. Like a rider on his horse, Jameson swung his rope without hesitation. When he swung by close to the ground the undead noticed him and immediately followed him. And as the rope took Jameson up in the other tree, the undead lost track of him and slowed down. At the time, we did not have any more ropes to continue drawing the undead's attention to move them further away. But Jameson had the guts to be the first rope-rider."

"Did you get rid of the undead at the time?"

"No, but a few days later their attention was caught by something and they moved away. But we learned how to continue building the sky road and made adaptions to benefit the rope-riders throughout the sky road."

"Wise move, but hadn't you figured that out already?"

"No, it was not a detail I remembered in the beginning, but as Jameson swung, it came back to me. I had seen the constructions, but not understood them nor paid enough attention to them at the time."

Controlling the undead in reality

You would imagine that Jameson were a true hero, a name for the history books. But the truth is far sadder. Jameson signed up to do some construction for a short period of time. His wife was expecting, and they needed the money. So, he left home for what would be a short while, a few weeks, a month at the most, and then he would head back home to be present when their first born would arrive.

But about a week after he left, he got word that both his wife and child were lost when the labour started prematurely. In lack of anything to return to Jameson stayed and continued at the sky road project. When they were stuck on the platform above the undead, Jameson figured he had nothing to lose. He had an idea, and if it worked, he would swing between the platforms and arrive safe on the other side, if not, he would join his wife and child on the other 'other side'.

Luckily for the others on the sky road, he arrived on the other side, and not the other 'other side', and he continued to work with them to build all that needed to be built. And continued to explore and perfect the art of swinging. Jameson was the first rope-rider, and for a long time, he was the greatest without match. His secret was not courage, but the desire to join his family. He pushed himself harder for every rope-ride, hoping that each swing would be the one that failed. Where all others were scared, he had hope and motivation. Where all others thought twice before they stepped of the platform only holding a rope in their hands, he stepped of the platform with peace and a calm mind, cleared of everything else and just focusing on the rope, the ground and the undead.

What Jameson started was moving undead for our own purposes, to be able to continue working safely on the sky road. But eventually, the hordes became greater and needed to be controlled. Not only not to cause harm to others, but also to act as some sort of camouflage to the sky road. If the ground beneath the sky road was often passed by undead, it was more likely that others would select

another road and minimizing the risk of detecting the sky road.
Which suited the whole sky road project just fine.

The plan forward according to Roy

"I have to say I am curious on what you plan on doing next, once you meet up with the others?"

"Naturally, I have thought a great deal about it. And our conversation has made me question the plan already. I was planning on joining the others, leading them back to the sky road in hopes to use it to get as far away from whatever is about to happen around here. But now, ten different forces at hand. All with different agendas. If we could eliminate, or at least significantly decrease the threat from the vampires and the undead it would be an amazing start. So that is where I now think we should start. And at the same time, the dwarves might need help, and should their army stumble upon any of the others, I doubt that an armed conflict can be avoided, not so much because of the dwarves, but rather the others."

"You say our conversation has made you think differently about your actions in the future?"

"Well yes, I thought I had a good plan, but now I am not so certain…"

"And in your plan, you figured you'll lead the others to safety and continue your life where you left it? Do you think the others agree on just following you? Or do you think they have opinions of their own, that may not be according to your plan?"

"Now I am even more confused. I have only thought from my own perspective. What I believe is best for the group. I mean, for the first time in my life, or rather once again in my life, I do not know anything about the future, not counting the bits and pieces I have gotten today. And from what I can read from your questions and what you say to me, between the lines, you know a lot more than you say and regardless of my plans and preparations it is more likely that something else will be."

"That is one way of putting it. And I have said too much about the future already."

"But not enough about the past."

"Well, from one perspective, the past can also be your future, so I will walk carefully as we speak. Perhaps even more careful than I have been up until now."

"I see…"

Roy sat quiet for a while before he continued.

"If you don't mind me asking. How long do you plan to stay here and chit chat with me?"

"Oh, a while longer, if I may. I find it very interesting to hear your thoughts and stories. And as long as you want to share, I want to listen. If you want me to leave, then just say the words and I'll be gone."

"No, I do enjoy you company. And as you probably can tell, I also do like to share my stories."

"No, really? Do you like to share your stories? I could not tell…"

"Now you are just pulling my leg, I know it, I can see a tiny smile in your eyes even if you try to hide it!"

The Wizard could not hold it any longer and laughed out loud.

"There is no fooling you, dear Roy."

"I guess time gives you that. Perspective and to see what is hidden in the little details."

"How right you are. It is often the small insignificant details that matter the most."

"How about a story with tiny details?"

"A story with tiny details, please entertain me!"

The plan forward in reality

Roy's entire plan forward had only two goals.

Pick up right where he left. Get away from danger.

Nothing more, nothing less.

And two things scared Roy.

Not knowing what would happen next. Many armies of infinite dangerous situation that could harm anyone in the group, or something worse.

Even if it was a new group of people he never met before, he felt drawn to them, destined if you will. And a longing of being part of something greater. Not that he hadn't accomplished great things in the ages that he had already lived, but he could feel that this was a special point in history.

Given everything the Wizard had spilled regarding his future, he was certain that he would be around much longer, which suited him just fine since he was afraid of dying.

But as for his other hope. Dee. Still uncertain. The Wizard had not spilled anything regarding her. Not yet anyway, even if Roy had a thought or two as to where some things were going.

Stuck in a cage according to Roy

"Little details… that is something that have saved me many times. Like once, where I was captured and put in a cage. Not a very pleasant experience I'd say. But nevertheless, there I was, stuck in a cage, for no apparent reason."

"No reason whatsoever?"

"Well… no… I mean, I just happened to be at the wrong place at the wrong time, that's all. But that's beside the point."

"And the point being?"

"As I was sitting there in that cage, about half my height, and equally wide on the other sides, I noticed little details in the construction of the cage. Details I could use to my advantage. This and the details of the guards, their movements, and changes in guard rotation and in their personalities."

"Sounds like a lot of details."

"Yes, exactly my point. Every detail mattered in my escape!"

"Escape? Did you break out of the cage?"

"Of course, I was held there on baseless accusation and against my will."

"Baseless accusations?"

"No, I don't want to get into that right now, I want to talk about the details."

"Then by all means, please do!"

"First of all, the cage. Not made by the dwarfs I can tell you. Sloppy work. Each time I moved around in the cage, which I had to do a lot since I could not find a comfortable way to sit, the hinges to the hatch slid slightly apart and back again. But on the locked end, it was totally fixed. I figured that with enough force I could get the hatch open on the hinge side. And given the rotation of the guards, and especially one who were particularly bored and always stood with his back towards the cage, trying to catch what others were saying through a window of a nearby bar. And tried to catch a glimpse of the barmaid, which he got the chance to do quite often."

"A given diversion…"

"Yes, so I also had to notice the patterns in the guests by the bar. Their behaviour affected the barmaid's behaviour and her behaviour affected this guard. And my plan was simple. Time my forcing of the hatch at a time where she would be serving at the table closest to the window, when she was bending slightly over to reach the far end of the table, that is when my guard was the most focused on her."

"Ah, the female enchantment."

"And I had to time it to sit in a certain position to get as much force as possible in one particular corner of the cage. And as she leaned over, I applied all the force I could find, the entire cage squeaked, and I managed to get the hinges to slide open and catch the hatch and keep it closed as the guard turned to look at what caused the noise. As I had calculated, he was not to observative and wanted to turn his attention elsewhere as quick as possible. Now I had only to wait until the next time she would serve the guests by the window table, so I could open up the hatch and make my escape."

"Did you?"

"Yes, without any obstacles on the way."

"Impressive. And yes, the importance of details."

Stuck in a cage in reality

No, Roy was not at all at the wrong place at the wrong time, at least not from a 'getting caught' perspective. He was where he intended to be, at a time he had planned, doing something that he also had planned, and got caught and put in the cage until the right authority could judge and administer the right punishment.

And as for the details, they were added to the story a long time after the whole situation, however, not fabricated only remembered and adapted to give the story a more powerful context. And even if only remembering the details afterwards, the whole situation still leads to a valuable experience for the future.

The whole getting the hatch up was an accident that were used wisely, totally improvised, and the escape was planned only after the hatch had opened.

In fact, Roy had to sit in the same position an entire evening to hold the hatch in place, in hopes not to raise suspicions from the guard.

The plot succeeded, and Roy managed to escape that time as well, as many others before, and many more to come.

Never have there existed any other that have made his way out of tricky situations and escaped out of punishment more times than Roy.

In his defence, we need to add that Roy have existed way longer than any other. But to contradict that, he still has escaped and dodged more during another person's lifetime than that person did during his or her own lifetime. Yes, I mean the same period of time, equal amounts of summers and winters.

Convincing the mayor to build the treasure rooms according to Roy

"Speaking of details, I have discovered that I have a wonderful memory for details. I can often think back to a situation or a place and keep recalling details from that moment in time even if I have not actively taken them in during the episode that created the memory."

"What I would say is more impressive than you are having a great memory for details, which in itself is very impressive, is that you seem to be able to store and process much more information and memories in that tiny brain of yours."

"How do you mean?"

"Well, you have a normal human brain, a thing that is designed to last the normal lifespan of a human. And sometimes the brain starts to decay while the human is alive, which is why old people can sometimes forget things and be very confused about a lot of things. But your brain, have been around for ages, and seem to work better and better as time is passing by. Must be an effect of the higher balance of life essence in your body…"

"I wonder how that will work out for Dee then… I believe she got a much bigger dose of the life essence than I did…"

"You will find out, eventually. Or, rather, I did not say that, I mean, time, from your perspective, may give you that answer, if you are around to experience it."

"…around to experience it…" Roy mumbled to himself and continued: "…you know one time I was fortunate to be working for the mayor of a newly founded city. He was only elected mayor because he recently had inherited a great deal of money from his late father and from his father's brother. Both killed by the elected mayor, which of course was not known by others. I convinced him to build a treasure room beneath the city, so he could expand his richness and keep the treasures hidden for anybody but himself."

"Clever, direct a greedy person with power to gain more wealth and power."

"Yes, and I got to spend time there as well. Room by room was finished, and each finished room were filled with various treasures. One of my favourite rooms were a gift from a human wizard that created a tiny world of glass, complete with an entire ecosystem including little beings that lived inside it…"

"Impressive power for a human wizard!"

"Yes, I believe she was called Leola, and considered to be a high-ranking wizard within the wizard and witch community. Even among other humans she was famous and well respected."

"Ah, Leola, yes, I have heard of her. Do you know that she is still around?"

"No, it can't be, then I would probably have run into her. I mean, immortals are not very common."

"You will son, eventually. That much I can give you."

"Huh, so now you want to share information about my future… how come?"

"Not saying, you need to find out for yourself."

"Ok, be cryptic, I don't mind! Anyway, the mayor, he was not around to see the treasure rooms finish."

Convincing the mayor to build the treasure rooms in reality

The only reason Roy got to work for the mayor was that he knew the mayors secret and threatened to reveal it. But the mayors first reaction was to try and eliminate Roy, so, Roy did what he did best, lied, hustled and deceived. He tricked the mayor into believing that Roy had a network of safety guards and that if he at any time failed to make his regular check-ins, the word would spread. That lie provided Roy with regularly funded travels to wherever he wished to go. And Roy made sure to travel in style with all expenses paid by the mayor.

But he did not want to be ungrateful towards the mayor and often offered to treasure hunt for the mayor whenever he was out on journeys. This also partially true. The treasure hunting was part for the mayor, who appreciated Roy's services, but also to extend his visits as Roy sent correspondence to get the mayors opinions of his findings before bringing anything back.

Some items he already knew that he should purchase for the mayor, since he had already seen them in the treasure rooms he once visited. Others he needed to verify the mayors liking.

And back home in the city, Roy oversaw the building and making of the complex underground treasure rooms with clever construction ideas that he remembered from his visit. The main architects were stunned with his ideas and often had a hard time to realize his input, but always manage to find the right material, calculate the needed structure and make it happen. All to the mayors liking. He had something no one else in the entire world possessed. Something that he held more valuable than the dwarf treasure chambers.

And in the end, the mayor's violent past caught up with him and he was beheaded by his adversaries whom he previously had tried to vaporise, both politically, economically and personally. Neither fronts were appreciated by the receivers.

The book-travelling man according to Roy

"Sad to hear, he started off with a vision and did not stand around to see it finish…"

"Well, let's just say that he had it coming. And speaking of treasures, have I told you about a very rich man I once met?"

"A rich man? Richer than the mayor?"

"Yes, and no. Yes, a lot richer in life, but not in money or physical things. He travelled with his mind."

"Ah, a wizard then?"

"No, not at all, he was like any other man, lived poorly, had barely enough to get food on the table."

"And still he could afford to travel?"

"No, not physically, but using his mind. He bought and traded books. And every book he could get his hands on, regardless of title or topic or type, he consumed it. Not just read it like most people would, he consumed it from the first letter to the last. Explored every detail of it closely."

"He used his books to travel in the mind?"

"Yes, through the details and descriptions in the books, he used his imagination to broaden his awareness and his experiences of various things, without ever leaving his home."

"A book-travelling man then…"

"Ha! Yes, that is the best word I have ever heard, and it describes him perfectly. A book-travelling man!"

"I just made it up, I don't think it exists."

"Well, now it does, and it means exactly the thing this man did! Brilliant word!"

"And in what way was he richer than the mayor?"

"In views and experiences. Of course, most of his experiences were made up and never actually experienced, but he had such rich views of a variety of things and subjects and could easily fall into dialog and discussions regarding anything and totally adapted to the person he was conversing with."

"A social chameleon?"

"A social what?"

"A kind of lizard that can adapt to its environment to stay undetected and blend in."

"I don't know about that, he adapted alright, but never undetected and certainly did not blend in."

"Why is that?"

"For one thing he was passionate about everything. You know that fire some people have when they talk about something they care about really deeply? He had that fire always. He was passionate about life, yet he never lived it in reality, he only read about it."

"Sounds a bit sad really."

"Well, yes, in a way, but he was happy, really happy. And nothing could take that away from him."

"And from that perspective he was richer than the mayor."

"Yes, so much richer than the mayor."

The book-travelling man in reality

This is in all a very sad story. Had it been a person that was attracted to stories and for that reason consumed each and every book for entertaining purposes, it had been a beautiful story with a deep message about not needing to be trapped in the material world, being a material being, pursuing material richness'.

But the sad truth is that this man did not live in the material world at all, he believed that what he was reading was true. His own experiences. And what we call the real world, he thought of as a strange place that kept pulling him back from his real life.

He was, in every perspective a mad man, harmful to no one, alone, seeking company in the strange world he found himself lost in. Eager to share his experiences and views to get help to return to his real world. But no one could ever give him directions on where to go or explain to him where he was.

Often, he returned to a familiar sad place in this strange world where he often, somehow and luckily, found his way back to his ordinary life again.

Always, he was alone, but for short periods where he had company of a few strangers that he got to know really well, each time in hopes that they this time would stay with him and forge deep lasting friendships. But he was always disappointed and continued in his loneliness his entire life.

No one attended his funeral, no one cared what was written on the stone. Hadn't it been for a friendly anonymous donor, he wouldn't have gotten any stone at all. But faith, it seems, smiles on this poor man, for many are those who stop at his gravestone and pay him a thought and a warm smile.

"Here rests a man who no one knew,
a man noticed by few.
Words and pages lead his way
to this place, where he will stay.
No longer lost among human souls
No longer lost in his changing roles.
A long and lonely life it took
To reach the last page, in his own book."
-R

The four-armed people according to Roy

"I bet you have met quite a few strange beings over the years. Haven't you?"

"Yes, indeed, quite a few…"

"What would you say was the strangest, or most difficult to meet?"

"I'd say that the strangest are equally the most difficult, and it definitely was the four-armed people."

"The four-armed people? Never heard of them!"

"Nor have I, but I met them. And it was actually one of my strangest over all experiences."

"Do share, dear Roy, I am thrilled to hear another story!"

"I was asleep, and when I woke up, I were no longer in my bed, I lay in a pile of sand, and everything was coloured by the red light from the sky. There was no sun nor clouds, but the light still felt like daylight. Felt like an entirely different world."

"Maybe it was!"

"What do you mean?"

"The less you know…"

"Alright, I'll pretend I did not hear that either. Anyway. The air was very dry, had never felt anything like it before. At first, I thought it was a dream of some kind, but I did not wake up. Instead, I was approached by a person with four arms. He, or she, I am uncertain, yelled something at me and I did not understand a single word. I rose and as I did the being stopped in front of me, kind of blocking way forward. It was kind of an odd gesture because I stood in what looked like a desert land, sand as far as my eyes reached in every

120

direction. Yet the sand did not seem random and unstructured as I had seen in deserts before, this sand seemed structured, almost crafted."

"How is that possible? Sand is volatile, impossible to structure if you ask me…"

"I know, I share your point of view, but none the less, this sand was structured, and I apparently stood in the middle of something that was not intended for standing. In front of me was this being, who I mistook for a human at first. Looked about the same as me, only angry. That was very clear."

"You did not see any extra arms?"

"No, they were hidden behind the back at first, and the being did not show them until I tried to move. At first, I tried to my right, that was when it threw out the second arm on its left side. Slightly bigger and longer than the first left arm that I already had seen. It was waving both left arms up and down and was clearly annoyed with my attempt in moving right. So, I tried to my left, and the whole scene repeated itself again, only a little more annoyed."

"And this was the first time you saw all four arms."

"Yes, and I was starting to expect more arms or legs to be revealed, or an extra head or something, but it stopped here, four arms, that was all."

"And two bigger and longer than the other?"

"Yes, and stronger I might add. When I tried to take a step backwards, it grabbed me with all its arms and lifted me straight up, over its head and put me down behind it before turning around facing me again. Unbelievable strong, bendable and flexible arms. Have never seen anything like it!"

"Fascinating!"

"And terrifying! I tried to start over and tried to greet it by reaching for its right bigger arm to shake its hand while I presented myself as 'Roy Hicks' and put my hand on my chest. It got furious and started to wave all four arms around and pushing me and knocking me over and over until I lay on the ground. I think it knocked me out completely, the next thing I remember is waking up where I started, in my own bed, completely beat up with bruises and all."

The four-armed people in reality

*Totally off subject, but Roy was right, it was another world.
Affected by his repeated encounters with the Wizard, Roy
unintentionally adapted some of the Wizards abilities. Like moving
from one world to another in an instant. Like crawling through time
rifts. Like… yes, you are right, off topic, I am sorry… sometimes I
get carried away. I will keep to the subject.*

*The four-armed people. Easily offended. When Roy extended his
right arm in the direction of the creature's bigger right arm to
shake its bigger right hand, it took it as a hostile move and reacted
accordingly, just as it had done when finding Roy in its delicious
pile of sand where the finest minerals crisped in the warm, dry air
of this world. Binding what little dampness the air could spare.*

*In fact, the four-armed people were very picky with gestures and
particularly sensitive when it came to interact with their arms and
hands. They have strict social rules as to what is acceptable with
which arm and which hand. And of course, Roy managed to offend
this particular creature by breaking many social rules and acted far
beyond any socially acceptable boundaries of this world.*

*Roy should consider himself lucky to only be beaten half to death.
But at the time, he didn't know all this, but he learned it later on in
his long and strange life. When this happened, he was only the
beginning of his eventful and unnatural life. Poor Roy (at that
time), if he only knew what waited on him further down the road…*

Hickston according to Roy

"Still, you made it out alive."

"Yes, probably thanks to my enhancements from Groll…"

"Maybe, but you strike me as someone with a lot of will to live. That is also very helpful, not only in surviving, but in living as well… anyway, I was thinking… have you ever accidently used your knowledge of the future to unintentionally help someone or change the course of events?"

"Do you have time to think during my stories? Am I boring?"

"No, my brain just works in different ways than yours, like this is one part of the multiverse that has its own complex chain of events like we discussed earlier, my brain handles several complex chains of thoughts in many different angles, time aspects, and so on. So, if you have a brain, I have a multibrain…"

"Oh… I see, but really I don't, just being polite I guess…"

"If you want to be polite, how about answering my question?"

"Of course, I can do that. I wasn't aware of this for a long time, and then one day I remembered something from my childhood, and I had to check it. But yes, one time I believed unintentionally changed the course of actions…"

"And what would that be?"

"I remembered once, on my way between one life and another, I passed a settlement of new builders. They had found a place near a river on a beautiful slope on the foot of a mountain. They had started to build a couple of wooden buildings. As I passed by, they offered me an opportunity to stay and help develop the settlement. They needed strong men to help them build, but they laughed and said that they would settle with me, if I was willing to give them a hand. Naturally I wasn't interested, even if they were a merry bunch. However, I pointed out, since I recognised the place from my childhood, that there would be a small sea just where they had started their construction. I pointed out that if the river would flood or be expanded in any other way, their new houses would be in the middle of water. They only laughed at me for saying so, but we still had a good time and parted as friends."

"Did it flood?"

"Yes, eventually it did. And the village is now called Hickston. I remembered it from when I was a child, because I thought it was strange to have a village that carried my name. And I investigated it once, but it turns out that one of the settlers was called Raymond Hicks, and the village is named after him, not me, even if theoretically could have had an impact on the town before it was built."

"But it wasn't your name?"

"No, sadly not…"

Hickston in reality

But in reality, it was named after Roy Hicks, and not the settler Raymond Hicks, even if historical documents said it was named after Raymond. The first documents clearly state that after they had finished their first houses, they decided to listen to Roy and built all other houses and concentrated their infrastructure to centre around another place, out of harm's way if anything would occur. And they did not have to wait long, the very next summer there was a shift in the mountain and the river flooded, creating a little sea around the first buildings. After that they unanimously voted to name their new town Hickstown after the stranger Roy Hicks that passed through. But later historians never found any records of a Roy Hicks in Hickston, so they wrongly assumed that Roy Hicks was the nickname of Raymond Hick, who was one of the first habitants of Hickstown. But Raymond arrived after the name was given, but again modern historians missed important details and made false assumptions. Then again, details are like truth, a perspective. But more about that later. Roy was recognized by the founders of Hickstown who over time became Hickston but as many other cases, the right person or the right fact or detail was not recognized by those who followed, and the real story was lost in history. While wrong assumptions and made up connections lay the foundation of the modern world and societies rules. Written and unwritten.

It is said that the winner writes the history, but not even that is completely true. The historians draw the history based on their assumptions of various doubtable sources. It might not be true all the time, everywhere, but in this world, it is far too common and far to unknown. Which is scary since history is always part of the path that leads forward. And if the path behind is not what it is said to be, choices of the future is based on wrong information and leads to a different place than first intended. Then again, the future is always unwritten, regardless of the past, and each decision, however it is made, gets its own consequences. Nothing right or wrong. Just different results of different choices.

Sorry, I am rambling on… Back to the story….

Inside the sea monster according to Roy

"Do you have any more monster stories? I like your monster stories…"

"I have at least two that I can think of. The one where I was shipwrecked and stranded inside the belly of a huge sea monster, and the one where I was caught surrounded by dragon's fire…"

"Begin with the sea monster, if you would be so kind?"

"Certainly, the first is back at the sea, but not beneath the surface, but on it. I travelled by a small boat along the coastline due south. It was when I was making a big leap between lives and would start over at the south. Fastest way down was by boat. But we were caught in a storm and the boat wrecked against underwater cliffs. Only me and one other survived and we managed to gather debris in the water and make us a floating raft. Of course, I could have managed by going under the surface again, but if Jonah also survived, it would be hard to explain how I had survived, so I stayed at the surface with him. This was during the time after the wizard war when the great witch hunt was at its peak, and I did not want to have the slightest suspicion of being a witch with supernatural powers, or worse, a wizard."

"That is a part of your history I want to hear more about, but we can save that for later. Sorry for interrupting, please continue."

"Well, there we were on the raft, no land in sight. And all of a sudden there came the largest sea creature I have ever seen… at first we thought it was some sort of island with a huge cave on one side, but pretty quick we realized that the cave was a gigantic mouth that stood wide open, ready to swallow us as we drifted inside, without means to control our bearing. And we drifted far inside the beast before it closed its mouth around us. Fortunate for us, or at least one of us, was that with its mouth shut, it preserved a great deal of breathable air inside its body as it submerged trapping us inside."

"Sounds horrible. How did you manage to get out?"

"Every now and then, the creature surfaced and opened its big mouth again. I am not certain, but I believe it had to do so to be able to breath, and that the air inside it was like when we hold our breath to be able to swim beneath the surface. Anyway, every time it opened its mouth, we tried to paddle our way out, but we never even got close. That's when Jonah got an idea. We split our raft in two, linking the two smaller rafts with a rope. And on the other raft we gathered as much debris we could find and piled it up as best as we could, then we set the pile on fire."

"Set it on fire? Inside the monster?"

"Yes, brilliant idea it turned out. The sea monster had to surface and had great trouble in getting the fire out of it, must have hurt terrible but it spit us out with tremendous force. As it did, the fire was flooded by a wave from the spitting monster, and the fire was put out. It almost leads to us being dragged in again, but it probably saw us as terrible food and we were successfully shut out of its big mouth on the drift in freedom again."

"I almost feel sad for that poor thing."

"The feeling is mutual, we did not take pride in the escape, and we promised each other to never tell anybody what we had done."

"Still you are telling me now…"

"Yes, I have never told this story to anybody before, and I wouldn't have either, if it weren't my travelling companion's betrayal. I heard our story told by others by a campfire shortly before I came here. But at least he had the decency not to include me in it…"

Inside the sea monster in reality

This is also an occasion where the story wasn't fabricated. But I can add that the inside of a sea monster is not a particularly pleasant place to be.

Imagine this; it is a very hot day, the sun is high on the sky, the wind has stopped leaving the air completely still. You are out minding your own business, and all of a sudden you are captured and put in a huge barn. A barn ten times bigger than any barn you have ever seen before. Or rather twenty times bigger. It is completely dark. The floor is covered with water, but not pure water. Water filled with piss, crap and puke. And soaking in this floating filth is pieces of rotting animals marinating. Air completely still, heavy and thick with smells worse than you just imagined. Not a pleasant place to be. Roy and Jonah had to feel around in this mess to try and find more debris to use in their escape. All in completely darkness. You would not imagine how hard it is to be in that smell and yet defy all-natural urges and keep searching in the disgusting pothole you are in. I bet you are thinking, how could they make fire in an environment like that? The answer is simple. Any sailor at this time had to carry firestones in their clothing at all time. Should it be dark and cloudy, and the lanterns was put out by the wind, their life could very well be depending on lightning those lanterns again. So, in this case both gentlemen was well capable of making fire, but neither had the urge to do so, both from the point of view to harm the creature, even if that was the smaller of their concern regarding the fire. But the most terrifying aspect of creating a fire was that it would shed the darkness around them, and neither was very keen on seeing the things that caused this awful smell, nor what they had been digging through with their bare hands.

Dragons fire according to Roy

"What about the other story including a monster?"

"It's about a fierce dragon."

"Oh, dragon, lovely, do share!"

"Twice in my long life I have experienced the mountain crumbling, shaking and bleeding."

"Uhm, the mountain bleeding?"

"Yes, ground shaking, mountain trembling with pain, heavily exhaling with dark dust and tiny rocks, bursting wounds with hot mountain blood pouring down its sides as the entire mountain hurts."

"I think you should spend some time with the dwarves and learn some basic mountain knowledge…"

"Do you want to educate me or hear the story?"

"The story please."

"Well, I was at a village once when a fierce dragon attacked a mountain. The mountain did not stand a chance. At first, we did not understand what was happening, we had not seen the dragon. We only felt the ground shake and then saw the dark clouds that the mountain exhaled. It did not take long until we saw the blood flowing down towards us. It floated slowly, burned everything in its path. It gave us time to seek refuge on a rock-solid hill that stood up from the other ground around us. Apart from a smaller hill next to ours. As the blood reached the foot of our hill, we saw the dragon. It came in hard and fast and attacked the other hill with its furious fire. Over and over again. Eventually the entire hill was consumed, and the mountain blood flowed slow over the fresh wound, as if the mountain were licking its newest wound."

"Sounds like an unprovoked attack by the dragon…"

"Yes, my point exactly. The still and harmless mountain. Defenceless by any definition. Brutally attacked by a dragon, or several dragons, what do I know? Leaving the mountain in pain and agony, bleeding. Our whole village was obliviated and we were lucky that once the mountain blood had livered a little and cooled down a little, we could follow a narrow path down the mountain where our hill had successfully divided the blood flow in two. Like splitting a river."

"And on what ground do you think the dragon, or the dragons if you say, attacked the mountain?"

"I have no idea, but dragons, I tell you, awful creatures the lot of them!"

"I just don't see what reason anybody would have attacking a mountain?"

"Maybe pure stupidity? What do we know what dragon thinks?"

"You do remember that it was Groll and Rueen that created the dragons, don't you?"

"Well yes, I do, but I never quite understood why. And turning against the creation the way they did, I have not understood that either."

"Perhaps they did not turn against the creation, maybe it is your understanding of it all that is impaired with your fear of what you don't understand?"

"What is there to understand about dragons? Nothing. Pointless, stupid and harmful beings!"

Dragons fire in reality

I don't know if it is obvious, but at this time, and for a very long time, Roy is terrified of dragons. But he will not always be afraid of dragons. There will come a time when he will care deeply for dragons. Maybe not dragons in general, but a specific dragon. A golden dragon. But when this dialog occurred, Roy was not to positive about dragons.

He claims that the dragon attacked the mountain, and that it was the dragon that caused the lava to erupt from the mountain. Of course, this is not true, it was just a volcano that had a tiny eruption.

But the dragon did melt that smaller hill with its furious fire.

Why, you might think, but in reality, it was pretty obvious to the dragon. That little hill would alter the flow of lava down the mountainside. And it would have two devastating consequences if it did. The first consequence was that the lava would trap those who had searched refuge on the higher hill, Roy included. The second would be a village further down the mountain. Even if the dragon was not sure that the lava would make its way entirely down the mountainside, it had to make sure that this eruption did not paralyse life in general. One of its strongest urges was to keep life safe. After all, the dragons are a creation of Groll and Rueen and their heritage is a strong force, even inside dragons. Despite attempts made by certain dragon trainers to tame their potentially destructive forces for their own purposes.

But history have shown, and will show again, that dragons are not to be tamed, they are their own masters and follow only their own will. But will gladly fight for life and the creation if asked to do so.

Life lesson according to Roy

"Well, enough of monsters… You have lived for a long time, if you could, what would your advice the mortals you have encountered throughout your life be?"

"Oh, a great many things I guess…"

"Like what?"

"Like anybody can achieve anything. If you want to be good at something, do it, hours on end, over and over again. Eventually you will be good at it. The average person wants to do something, practice a bit and become good at it. Most people stop here. Those who put in more time and effort will master it… Again, a lot of people stop here. Those who keep pushing themselves perfects themselves to an unimaginable level. Those who reach this level stop competing with others and only compete with themselves to do it better and better each time."

"So, anybody can learn to do anything, even without skills to begin with?"

"I guess, I have not really thought about that, but I assume as much. Spend time on what you like doing, and eventually you will learn. I mean, from what I have seen everybody sets their own limits. There is nothing in this world that is out of reach, but we are all taught limits and rules as children, first by our parents and other adults, then in school and by society, all unwritten social rules. Most people accept those boundaries and stay within the limited space it permits. Out of comfort I would imagine. And it's nothing wrong with that. But they are really invisible and imagined fences. Nothing but our own mind keeps us trapped behind them. Some break free but only expand their fences and push the boundaries a little further out. Life becomes very different when you do that. And very few realises that there are no fences or limits at all. They can live completely free. To many this freedom is freighting and if they have discovered that there are no fences, and are frightened of it, they tend to rebuild their limits and stay behind that invisible fence."

"You are quite deep, my friend. I must say that I am quite moved with your words. And honestly I did not think you had a side like this…"

"How so?"

"Well, it is easy to judge a book by its cover, to see a ragged dog if the fur is tangled and filthy."

"A ragged dog?! Is that supposed to be a compliment?"

"Perhaps a compliment in disguise."

"Very well disguised in that case…"

"What I am saying is that you took me with surprise and have affected me on a deep level. Believe it or not, but I too have lived behind invisible fences, but you have opened my eyes and I believe I can rise to new levels. Get out on a completely new arena… Who would imagine that an upgraded mere mortal could teach an omnipotent being like myself lifechanging lessons?"

"Now that is a complement!"

"Your welcome and thank you for your lesson!"

Life lesson in reality

Believe it or not, but Roy actually had a deep impact on the Wizard, and it had a deep impact on the entire multiverse. And since the Wizard lives and acts outside of time, the changes echoed throughout time, from Roy's and his fellow humans' perspective. A change that Roy did notice, not right away, but over time.

In the Wizards defence, Roy was not known for his deep insights nor sharing or discussing them, so the Wizards surprise could definitely count as fair. But, and this is one of those times where a 'but' is necessary (most of the times 'but' is unnecessary and only confuses things). And the 'but' this time is that the Wizard knew Roy over time and knew that Roy always manages to surprise. And from that perspective, the Wizard should not be taken by surprise by Roy and always expect anything.

By the way, do you know what Roy called the Wizard once? After he was questioning Roy about several things he had tried to teach Roy, Roy said: 'you are not a Wizard, you are a Quizard'. Hilarious! Absolutely and completely... no? Well, I thought it was funny anyway. It's not my fault that you are humourless.

Ha! Got you! Did you really think that I could read your reaction a long time after I wrote these words and they got printed? Maybe I can? Maybe I'm like the Quizard? No, I'm not. But I could be, and that would have been awesome. But that is also a lesson, never make assumptions. Even if assumptions can be true most of the times, they might be very harmful and lead to terrible consequences when they are not true. I know that from own experience, but that is something for another time. Now, let's get back to what we are doing and continue with the conversation between Roy and the Qui... sorry, Wizard!

Meeting captain Lars according to Roy

"Now that you have given me a lesson, have you at any time met anybody that has given you a lesson, something that you could pass on to others or something that you yourself could use?"

"Well, I guess plenty of times. Are you thinking of direct knowledge that I later could apply, or lessons that I later have learned when looking back at certain events?"

"Please share both, and even if the second sounds far more interesting, I would like to start with some example of the first, if you don't mind?"

"I do not mind at all, and the first person I come to think of is captain Lars. He had been at sea since he was a young boy and knew pretty much everything there is to know about travelling on the sea."

"And he taught you seafaring?"

"No, not at all, when I met him, he was given his first assignment as captain of a ship, and it was not just any ship. A brand new, latest in mechanical technology. At the time I was looking for someone to ship goods from the north to the south, preparing for another life and new beginning down south among the warmbloods."

"And captain Lars showed you the ship and its mechanical wonders?"

"Yes, he gave me the grand tour and showed me the benefits of all mechanical enhancements, changing the very nature of seafaring, cutting crew needs in half, and possible even lower. And this of course had several benefits. Less crew meant cheaper transport of goods, but it also meant significantly less space for crew supplies, giving more space for commercial goods."

"Sounds like he impressed you with the tour."

"Yes, and to my surprise I understood the basics of the mechanical technology he showed me, knowledge I later could use when constructing the sky road, and in many other occasions in various tricky situations."

"And captain Lars showed you all the mechanical things and shared his knowledge of mechanical technology?"

"No, I doubt that captain Lars knew much about mechanics. But he was a hell of a sailor. That is why they gave him the Glory. Even if it was his first assignment as captain and he was the first captain for the Glory the transporters knew he was the man for the job. The understanding of the mechanics just came to me as I got the guided tour and saw all the ropes, wooden wheels, and a lot of other things joined together in a mechanical harmony. I guess I just saw the harmony and could appreciate it."

"Basically, you self-taught yourself the basics of mechanics by looking at it on the ship?"

"In a way. It spoke to me, and I understood it. Maybe it was because it was so naked and open compared to other mechanical things I had seen previously. Every piece was connected to another and they all formed a unity, almost like a being. Each detail, a little piece of the whole, looking insignificant but important to the whole. One failed piece and the entire being was crippled."

"You speak of it as a living being, the ship I mean."

"Then you should hear captain Lars. He was not much for the mechanic part of it, other than its ability to perfecting his sailing, decreasing his crew and so on."

Meeting captain Lars in reality

The captain Lars Roy met was the first of the Lars' to captain the Glory. It was passed down in generations from father to son, until that faithful journey where she would deliver the silver egg from the south to the north, by the first captains' great grandson. Each generation of Lars' improving the ships mechanics and enhancing the Glory further. Perfecting her. After all, she was the pride of the trading fleet. And even if she had sister ships, she was their first, their best and the most known.

It was not entirely true that the first captain Lars did not know much about the mechanics, but he was sure not to focus too much on it, since it was fairly new to implement it on a ship to reduce crew and maximize goods capacity. He did not want to make the first customers suspicious of the technology, so he held a low profile on the mechanical talk with purpose.

Fate had it that Roy was involved and affected by the first and the last journey of the Glory.

And Roy was so impressed by captain Lars, and he came back as a passenger on the ship for his way down to the south. In fact, he is one of the few passengers on the Glory, throughout all her years of service. And one other would also cross Roy's path, not counting Rick who he soon would reunite with. The wizard, Leola. She once ordered transport of things from the south, delivered to Rick's and Dee's home village and demanded to see how the cargo was treated along the way. That journey lead to later modifications for a much more important cargo to be carried the same way.

Now, I just want us to be on the same page (which I really hope, since you are reading this in a book), when we here, at this time discuss technology and mechanics, we are far from what you call technology today, or mechanics today. At this time, it is only wooden pieces, stings and ropes that make out the entire foundation for the mechanical wonders of this time. There is no metal, no electricity, nothing digital or anything else you might expect from your point of view.

Truth according to Roy

"Another thing I learned, but only after a great while, was that there is no truth."

"Oh, this sounds interesting! I bet you are quite alone in claiming this."

"I have not talked to anybody about it, I have only realized it and carry with me this perspective to simplify my own life. And the paradox of it, is that if there is no truth, that can't be true either."

"You are teasing me and making me more curious, please explain."

"Ok, I need to give you a few background facts first, and as you know, a fact is an unquestionable truth that are accepted by most."

"Interesting definition, but I can agree with it."

"I have met and spent a great deal of time with Groll and Rueen. They are what this world refers to as the creator. They have created most life on this world. And I say most because I honestly don't know if they have created every lifeform or if there have been other sources of life here. At a later point in my life, I have spent some time with a few monks, claiming to serve the creator and acting as the creator's entrepreneur in this world. They had scrolls upon scrolls with the creator's words that they had received during various meditation sessions or other experiences. Their scrolls did reflect the thoughts of Groll and Rueen, but they still could not figure out that there were two creators. They kept referring to the creator as one being. If I now look past what I have learned from you today, which supports my claim even further, I concluded that even if the monks somehow could tune in to the entire creation, and get the right "information" from it, they still got things wrong. But the things they had written down was true in the perspective that they could verify most of the things with observations of the world around them, giving the spiritual part even more proof. From their perspective there are a single creator of this world and of the life

140

here. A single creator with a purpose in every action. They can verify this by looking at the balance in nature, find the perfection in nature and from their perspective their thoughts and truths are not wrong. From my perspective it is wrong. I know Groll and Rueen. Shure, they had a lot of good intentions and some general plan when creating life here, but they did not create this world, you did, and they told me you did. So, from my perspective the monk's theories were not true, but from their perspective it is true. And this is pretty much the foundation of my claim that nothing is entirely true. Even if you can see and verify your truth, there can always be another perspective proving your perspective incorrect."

"'Basically, you say that you and I can view the same thing and see different things and have two completely different versions of what we see, that are true to us both, but not entirely true to either of us, since the truth is not the same for us both. And your explanation is the perspective?"

"I'd say that you are a good listener, because that is exactly what I am saying."

"Then I need to ask you a question to this. You and I see the exact same thing, like this flower in front of us. And as I bend down and reach for it, picking it up, we both see the same thing. We see the flower growing on the ground, a hand reaching down, picking it, and holding it. Is that not a simple and absolute truth?"

"It might be, but I still claim that there could be other perspectives. Nothing that I can think of now, but I could argue that we could have different views of it. Yours could be that the flower is a gift of nature and yours to bring home to make your home more beautiful and get you closer to nature. I could claim that you are destroying nature and working against it by killing a beautiful flower in not letting it be. Removing it from its natural state and disrupting the life-flow of it."

"That is certainly the perspective of it, but doesn't that make the perspective of the truth not true and not the truth itself?"

"Uhm, well, maybe. But filtering the truth through a perspective, can we really see the truth?"

"Now that is an entirely different thing. The truth may or may not be there, but our perspective of it can be equally true to ourselves as it is untrue to somebody else."

"So, I am not wrong in my statement, but not right either?"

"That my friend, could very well be true."

"You mean, true-true?"

"Yes, I mean 'true-true'."

"But then I have another question. Let's say that there is an absolute truth. Can we ever see it without adding our perspective and filtering it?"

"I believe you just asked the right question, and in that question, you have your answer."

"Huh."

Time according to Roy

"Do you have more examples of when you have got insights sneaking up on you over time?"

"Good choice of phrasing, no pun intended."

"What do you mean?"

"Insights sneaking up on me over time… that was just what I was going to talk about. Time."

"Ah, I see…"

"Yes, and this is not really something that I have done, that I have learned something from, rather a lesson from time itself."

"Like you said before, I pretend I understand what you are talking about, in hopes that you will continue and eventually make sense."

"Well, let me put it like this. Before I became immortal, or at least not dying of old age, I did never reflect much about time at all. And as time has passed me by, a lot of time, because unlike you, I am stuck in time and cannot control it, only watch it pass me. I cannot save time, stop time, speed time up, grasp time or do anything with it, except live it."

"That is a new perspective…"

"Yes, and the more time that passes me by, the more I realise what I could have used it for."

"What do you mean?"

"I mean in every moment of time, I have a choice, I can do something, or I can do nothing. Doing nothing most often changes nothing and gives me nothing. While doing something most of the time has multiple outcomes. Which is also the hard part of it. There are a lot of somethings and choosing among them is hard. For a long time, choosing among all the options has overwhelmed me and lead to doing nothing, which has not made much good. But an inner sense of doing something and not just any something, but the right something has become overwhelming. The trick here is that when the moment comes, and the choice needs to be done, I have learned that you cannot spend too much time on choosing, because if you do, the moment has passed and is gone forever. That is another tricky thing about time, for us humans anyway, once a moment is gone, that is it. You cannot go back and make a different choice. Each choice is here and now, and if you make no or the wrong choice, you have to live with it and the potential consequences with it. And just to add to the complexity. Most often making no choice at all also have consequences."

"Sounds like it is tricky to live with time, to be limited by it."

"Yes, it can be, but it is also the beauty with life. We are all equal to time, no one have more time to spend or less time to spend, and we all have our own choices on how to spend it and have to live with the consequences of your own choices. Thus, I would say that time is what makes us humans rich. It is the only thing we have, and only thing we can spend, and no one can say they have more or less. Except for me and possibly Dee and Rick. Possibly the three of us have infinite time. So, I'd say that time is the only valuable thing we have. Not limiting us but helping us to fulfil ourselves. I for one have become very aware on what I spend my time on, even if I have a lot of time to spend, I do not want to waste it."

Thoughts and actions according to Roy

"And before you interrupt with another question, I can change subject to another important thing that I have been thinking a lot about."

"Sounds like you have been thinking of this a long time but have closed the thoughts inside of you, and now, all of a sudden you are eager to let them out, as if you no way possible could keep them inside any longer."

"You are right, and now you need to be quiet just a little longer and let me get this of my chest as well. I am thinking of thoughts and actions. If you only keep the perspective to one person, the person can have two types of thoughts, positive and negative. Regardless of it is about themselves or others. The positive thoughts are like clogs in a fire, it can make the energy and heat more intense, which is something I say to try and underline the positive effects of the positive thoughts. As for the negative thoughts, it can help to put out the fire and letting the cold inside. Which is bad. Now a second perspective to one person. A thought is always the first step of an action. And thoughts that does not become actions are like planted seeds that starts to grow but die because they dry out. A waste. A thought that does become action is a fulfilled thought and a seed that becomes a plant. If there is too big of a difference between thought and action a person is contaminated by the unfulfilled thoughts and the person starts to feel bad. Not physically, but emotionally bad. I've seen it several times, people feeling bad because they are not true to themselves. This is also true between two people. Only thoughts are replaced with words, since the thoughts needs to be communicated. And between two people, it is the power of the word that can get the fire of the relationship between the two brighter and warmer. Or, if the words do not match the actions, put the fire out and bring cold to the relationship. In this case words and actions need to be the same, actions without words or words without actions risk damaging, but when words and action are the same, it builds."

"Wow, you have indeed given this much thought!"

"Yes, and it feels good to say it out loud. Gives it more power and sets it in a bigger perspective. Also feels like it makes it truer."

"...and we know truth is a perspective, from what you said earlier..."

"Yeah, makes it a little harder to be happy about it... since I believe that my perspectives will always cloud me from the real truth, even how simple it may be."

"You are probably right, but don't underestimate yourself, or the wisdom given to you with time."

"How do you mean?"

"Well, as you probably know by now, a perspective will change over time."

"Certainly. Not only once, but it will continue to change, as time passes by."

"Yes, and you may have noticed that as the perspective changes, you tend to see things differently, and if the thing we talk about would be a spot on the ground, your changes in perspective will make you move from point to point around the same spot, in a circle. But not moving sideways in a circle one step at the time, no, more like jumping all over the place, standing in different places along the circle..."

"I can easily agree to that!"

"Do you know what will happen to your perspective as you have stood on all points around the circle with the spot in the middle?"

"No?"

"You have had every perspective surrounding that spot. Seen the spot from every single angle. That gives you all perspectives, and as you get all perspective, you can also see the spot as it truly is, without perspective."

"So, time will make the perspectives fade?"

"Yes, but it takes a lot of time, and most people do not have it! But you have!"

Truth, time, thoughts and action in reality

Truth as perspective, equal to time making the perspectives fade so the naked truth is revealed. Action that speaks louder than words. And the need to match thoughts and action.

It would be easy to look passed all this and only continue with the story, seeking the next moment of entertainment, but I cannot help but to hold on to these thoughts. They have followed me for many years, and over and over again I have returned to this conversation, to the ideas shared. I can honestly say that they have had a great impact of my life and have in a weirds way helped me in countless and various situations. Even if it is not some word of wisdom to cling on to and guide my steps along the path in front of me, it has been comforting and strong words to return to, time and again.

But what do you say, let's carry on with the next story. Leave these thoughts for now, maybe to return to them later, or just let them pass?

Meeting the Dhan according to Roy

"Even if I cannot entirely agree that what we now have discussed is good examples of knowledge that you have achieved directly from somebody else, I do see it from your perspective. Those were situations that you have acquired direct knowledge."

"Yes, thinking of it, I do not ever believe I have had a teacher or mentor that has guided me. The closest candidates are you in this situation and of course Groll and Rueen, whom have spent great deal of time with me, sharing their blessings with me, but not as teachers or mentors. More as friends or even family."

"Then how about situations where you did not gain the knowledge right away, but afterwards with perspective?"

"A few that I can think of straight up."

"Begin with the first."

"Throughout time there have been many conflicts between different human groupings. The groups and common denominator have shifted over time, but for a long time the way of the warfare did not. Always the same, a force of a number of fighting men, first by feet, then by horse, attacking the enemy. Bringing chaos to their homes, leaving with whatever they fancied. Money, animals, food, clothing, women, slaves, whatever they could lay their hands on and carry home. Then one day, there was a new pack leader in one of fractions. His name was Dhan. He had a different method and strategy than all the others. What had been clan positions inherited by blood band and birth right was now turned upside down by this former outcast."

"What did he do differently?"

"Well, for one, he recruited. Best man for the job got the job. It is said that he once recruited an arrow man from a village he attacked because the arrow man had shot him with an arrow in the neck. And once all men were rounded up the Dhan asked the defeated force who fired the arrow, he took a step forward and admitted it. The Dhan was impressed both with the man's courage and skills with the bow, so he gave him two choices. He said: 'A skilled bow-man who has the courage to take responsibility for his action does not do anyone good if he is dead. I'd rather use your talent against my enemies. As far as I am concerned your life is mine, but I want to give it back to you and hope you will serve with me as an equal.' Of course, the equal part was both true and untrue. The great Dhan gave all his loyal subjects the same treatment, in general good, but the punishment for disobedience was death. And you could be punished for somebody else's disobedience, if you served in the same unit. This particular bow man became a great general under the Dhan."

"What is your lesson in this?"

"Well, the Dhan recruited people with skills and awarded good work as opposed to traditional ruling amongst low life scum. With this strategy he employed many great people and made good use of their skills and differences."

"Did you ever meet this Dhan?"

"Twice, the second would have been my death if it weren't for his."

"Please share!"

"The first time I was passing through a village he attacked, I did not participate in the battle and when he rounded up all prisoners afterwards, I requested an audience."

"What did you say to him?"

"I said that I was just a stranger passing by, looking for food and temporary shelter for the night, and that I had no enemy in the great Dhan. He answered that he had no interest in why I was in the village, nor in my life. I replied and asked if he could have use for someone who spread the word of not only the fears warrior Dhan, but the just and good hearted Dhan who could separate friend from foe, and the wise Dhan who would spare anybody who was not in conflict with him. He thought for a while and then he let me go. And I kept my word and spread the word of kindness regarding the Dhan."

"So, the first time he spared you, what happened the second?"

"The second time was in the middle of the great plains. I was on my own, crossing it. I had heard rumours that the undead had taken over a town in the outskirt of the great plains, so I gambled to take a short cut. I had previously had encounters with slavers and was in a hurry to put some distance between me and them. And in the middle of the great plains, there he came riding with his men, the great Dhan. He immediately recognized me as the one he let go. Apparently, he later regretted that decision and saw it as a moment of weakness. But he had heard that I had kept my word and had spread the word about his kindness and goodness. Unfortunate for me, that wasn't the image he was going for, he wanted the world to fear him and respect him. He hesitated a little to give the orders to kill me. That's when it happened. An inside rebellion lead by one of his generals, a few of his men turned against the Dhan and they managed to kill him. Most of them lost their lives in the battle, but once the fight was over, the leading general declared himself as the new leader. And since he was inclined to be the opposite of the Dhan, he said that he would spare me and let the Dhan keep his first word to me, but also warned me that if our paths would ever cross again, he might not give me the same treatment again."
"You are one lucky man, Roy, you know that?"

"Yes, I have thought about it many times, and I have never been able to determine why…"

"Luck is nothing you can determine why. It is a force of its own. Cannot be controlled by man or life essence or forced by my hand. It is always without reach and acts on its own, with its own agenda."

151

Meeting the Dhan in reality

Ah, the great Dhan, no bigger warrior nor feared leader had excited up until that point. By your time perspective, the only who could possibly measure himself with the Dhan is the dwarf king Thidas. But you have only started to realize that he could be a problem. But in fact, he is the one dwarf that are solely responsible for bringing the dwarves to the dark ages.

But this was not supposed to be about Thidas, but the great Dhan. It is interesting how he got his name. Most people at the time of Dhan weren't able to read or write, but since he was a thrifty man, he recruited that skill. Only the one he recruited wasn't too good at writing. The Dhan was born with the name Bartholomeus, a name he could not stand. And when he started his quest to become the greatest and most powerful leader of all times, he figured he needed a new name. And he was aiming for the Dawn, but like I said earlier, the man who was supposed to write it down for him did not know how to spell the word, and it ended up being the Dhan. Which the Dhan never knew, since it sounded the same.

Well, enough about the background, Roy meeting the Dhan the first time. Roy was unlucky at the time and got caught in a place where he did not belong who happened to have the rage of the Dhan turned against it. That place and the people in it had defied the Dhan earlier in getting bad crops and not being able to pay the Dhan what he thought they owed him, despite the starving of the people.

Roy used his smooth mouth to talk his way out of the situation, as many times before, and to his surprise, it worked this time as well.

But faith is a peculiar fellow and connects random moments into a complex web of events, people and circumstances. One of the men that was recruited the day Roy got away, was the same general that started the rebellion that killed the Dhan. Which leads to the second time.

Should it not have been for the rebellion, Roy most likely would have died that day, despite his habit of not doing so. And death would not leave without a new prize, and since Roy yet again slipped through the fingers of death, death claimed another victim. A victim that had already provided death with plenty of work throughout the years. The end of the Dhan was a new dawn for Roy. He did not realize it at the time but learned the truth as the summers passed, joining the winters in between.

The tale of the great Christina according to Roy

"What about other historic people?"

"Plenty, not that I've met them all, but I have encountered a fair share…"

"Any who impressed you particularly?"

"This one is easy… the great Christina…"

"Who was she?"

"A strong-willed girl in a world dominated by men."

"Do tell…"

"She was fascinating in so many levels. Only daughter of a warrior king. Taught by her father from an early age to rule when he was too old. This was not liked among the king's competitors who wanted his throne. A girl to be their new ruler once the king died, unthinkable. But he had made his mind up, she was his heir. Sadly, the king died when Christina was very young, and she got a guardian to help her rule, until she was ready. She was a girl in a man's world. She was taught a man's view of women, she was taught war strategies, politics, economics, and many other things. Far from what she was supposed to be taught as a woman. No wonder she identified herself as a man and fell in love with another woman."

"A woman in love with another woman, have never heard of it!"

"It is far more common than you would imagine, men in love with men, women in love with women. I do not see it much stranger than a man in love with a woman, or the other way around. Love is love, that is all."

"I am sure you are right!"

"Anyway, as Christina got to the appropriate age to rule herself, to be the new king, her guardian wanted her to sign various papers and treaties to celebrate her first day as king and to prove that she was capable to carry the crown and fulfil her duty. But she wouldn't sign anything that day. She had made her own mind on how things should be and did not agree with the establishment that had grown in the absence of her father. She dismantled the establishment, piece by piece, all in fashionable order, and took control of every piece of business as any king would be expected to do. Man, or no man, no matter. She proved her worth as king, far beyond any expectations. In fact, she was such a great king that people forgot she was a woman. Her only flaw as king was to provide a new heir to the throne. It was the duty of each king to provide an heir. But since she did not want any man by her side, that was difficult. Thus, she changed the law so that the closes blood relative, in this case her cousin, could be the rightful heir to the throne, in the unlikely event that the sitting ruler did not have any first born. Of course, in this particular case, it was highly likely that she would not have any first born."

"It almost sounds like she planned this from the start."

"I believe she did. And as soon as the law was changed, she declared that she no longer wanted to be king, and handed over the crown to her cousin. She left the kingdom with her love, moved south to the warmbloods and perused art for the rest of her life. Passionate about art she was, I met her a few times. Skilled in the art of conversation as well, even if almost no one knew she was a former king from the north, it was easy understand that she was well educated and mastered almost any subject, and upon her death she was a poor old lady with nothing to her name. But even so, she was so well liked by the society, so they buried her like the king she truly was."

"Sounds like a beautiful tale. Too good to be true."

"Well, what can I say, sometimes truth is better than fiction."

The tale of the great Christina in reality

The tale of the great Christina sounds like Roy made the whole thing up. But he did not. This is a great summary of a very interesting historic event, even if, of course, Roy had made some artistic changes to give the story a deeper level of commitment from the listener.

The historic facts about King Christina from the cold kingdom in the north is documented in our history books, and if you fancy more sources on this, I recommend that you seek them out.

In fact, our history is filled with many great tales. Some more appealing than others, but the sense of it being true, or almost true (the winner writes the history books, we'll get to that later) the stories often gives me chills and goose bumps when reading. Highly recommend the reading experience. If not the history of the north, perhaps the history of your own surroundings, which ever they may be. I am sure there are quite a few historic records that will catch your interest. Or historic persons for that matter. But a little piece of advice. Don't dwell in the past too long. It is here and now we live and here and now we belong. No matter how great the past may seem or how appealing an untold future may seem, it is here and now, and only here and now, you exist and can act.

Art and Mina according to Roy

"Any other famous people?"

"I come to think of is Art and Mina…"

"Now, how are they, and why are they famous?"

"Well, they should not be famous, for one they were simple thieves who wasn't even good at that… and they were violent and dangerous, but somehow they rose to fame throughout their lives, even died in a famous way…"

"Sounds interesting, do tell!"

"Well, they grew up in a small village, both in poor families. Arthur Winsh and Minavera Leash. He was about two summers older than her, and it was only when Mina joined the child pack that Arthur turned to a skilled pickpocket thief. He wanted to impress Mina, who always knocked everybody with her beauty. Mina on the other hand enjoyed the thrill and danger of what Art was doing, and eagerly cheered on Art to continue his wrongdoings."

"It sounds wrong on so many levels that they reached fame and had a historic impact. I kind of hope that you are only pulling my leg right now."

"I'm not, I assure you, even if I myself would have a hard time to believe it, should I have not been there and experienced it myself. Pretty soon Mina did not find pickpocketing very amusing, and Art had to advance to heavier crimes. His first theft that was not pick-pocketing was stealing a rare horse called a mustang. It was breaded by a particularly great horse whisperer named Henry Mustang. His horses were particularly strong, had stamina far beyond any other horses and was particularly beautiful to the eye. Art stole the horse from a wealthy trader who was passing by their village and brought Mina with him on the ride. They took the horse and ran away from home that day. The first time they left their hometown, but not the last. They got caught and Art was thrown in jail, while Mina who was only with him on the ride got away. In jail Art did not behave particularly well, so he was sentenced to labour in the nearby woodcraft party. In chains as the rest of the prisoners. But Art did not plan on staying there for long, he wanted to get back to Mina and actually run away with her and give her all the riches of the world. But as a chained prisoner there was very few opportunities to escape. Thus Art, true to his Mina, he hurt his foot and leg deliberately to be able to get transferred to the doctor's quarters, where it was much easier to escape. Little did he know that his mother had pleaded for his release, and since it was rather crowded in the prison at the time, the law had agreed to release him. But when they tried to find him to give him the news he had already escaped from the doctor's quarters. And they figured that news had arrived to him sooner and that he had already been released. So, no one looked for him or questioned that he wasn't properly released. The injuries he inflicted on himself would haunt him for the rest of his life, he needed to ride barefoot on that side, could never wear shoes while riding."

"Faith has a strange way sometimes…"

"Indeed. And right after his escape, or being unknowingly released, he united with his Mina again, and kept on with their thievery."

"But what made them famous and why did people like them?"

"Well, many small things I guess, but one thing was that they always managed to escape, no matter how slim the odds of escape were, they found a way out. And Art was a really good painter, and he always painted him and Mina in various places, and the paintings were often left behind when they had to make a rapid exit of their current whereabouts. That is also why he got his nickname, Art. Even if it was short for Arthur, it was mainly because his painting talent. And strangely the paintings were sold at a very high price. He would probably have been able to make a living as an artist, had he chosen that path instead. Another thing that made them famous was that Art loved stealing Mustangs. He liked those horses so much that he at one point wrote a letter to Henry to thank him for his great horses."

"Sounds like they lived a life truly free…"

"In a way, they did as they pleased, when they pleased. But they also left a big trail of dead bodies as they kept on their never-ending thievery streak. Which made them quite unpopular by the law. But to common man the dead were often people that common man did not like, for one reason or another. People who made money of the poor, who used the system and the poor people for their own wealth. So, I guess that common man looked passed the trail of bodies and only saw the glamorous free-living couple that did as they pleased."

"How did it end?"

"In orderly fashion, an escape they did not make it out of. They were about to come home to meet their families, on a stolen Mustang, of course, and they had been sold out to the law by someone close to the families, who got quite the bounty for turning Art and Mina in. As usual they tried to escape, but this time they were vastly outnumbered and taken by surprise. Still they managed to bring down a few lawmen along with them. And as they died, the interest of them faded and nowadays I would be surprised to hear anyone talk about them or even know who they are if they saw one of Art's paintings."

"Sad story…"

Art and Mina in reality

Even at this time, people looked for heroes rather than thieves. But the common man found some poetic justice in a couple of poor people taking on the entire system and defy social structures and common sense, seeking to be something more than their birth right served them. Even with hard work it was hard to pass from one layer in society to another. And they did not accept to be poor and be bound by poor people's boundaries. They wanted more out of life and was not ashamed to take it. The only thing that talked against them was their violence, which most people would look through their fingers about, because the people who tried to stop them from achieving their goal in a way protected those who unfairly took things from common man without any reasonable or fair reason. That's just the way things were.

So, even if common man did not think that Art and Mina was acting right, they kind of romanticized it a bit and the public opinion turned down the horrors of their doings.

All and all, when they died, each pierced with countless arrows, leaving nothing behind except a planted seed that things could be different than what they are. Everybody can make a change, and anybody can initiate changes.

Their heritage became disassociated with themselves, because even if they were celebrities of their time, you simply cannot worship criminals who ruthlessly murdered other people. Unless, and again, we'll come to that later, you are the winner and write the history. Art and Mina did not win, it was not they who would write their history. So, the seed they planted, a seed that grew to the rising of the people, changing the society of the time, was never credited Art and Mina. It just happened. And maybe it would have, by itself, but I am pretty sure that Art and Mina at least was one of the sparks that lit the fire. Regardless of what our history books tell us.

The Witch-hunt according to Roy

"What about big events in your history? And what did you learn?"

"One thing in particular has affected me and scared me many times."

"What was that?"

"It was after the wizard war, it was a time that brought out the best in some people and the worst in others."

"How do you mean?"

"As for the worst, the general public blamed all wizards and witches for the war and the devastation it brought. Lack of food, houses and crops in aches, animals that had been so stressed out that they no longer provided milk nor offspring. They hunted down each and every witch they could find and burned them alive. But not only the real witches, sometimes an innocent person would be accused of being a witch, and they would be captured, tortured and burned alive as well. A time without law or common sense, a time where no one were safe, and everybody could get accused, from anyone. Friend, foe, neighbour and sometimes even family. Really a horrible time. There is no telling how many innocent men and women that were wrongfully accused and burned during the witch-hunt. But several thousand I imagine. As if the war had not caused enough loss, pain and suffering. Families that had survived the war were now torn apart, even more children lost one or both their parents. Some lost one in the war and the other in the witch-hunt. It was a time of total chaos and anarchy. Naturally, I kept very low profile during that time, as far as I know, I am not entirely safe from flames, and should it not kill me, I am certain that I would not have been released to lick my wounds... I imagine a much worse faith would await me if I did not die of the witch fires."

"Horrible, but what about the best in people?"

"At the same time when most people lost all common sense and ignored both written and unwritten laws, some stepped forward in the most humane way. With care, compassion and love. Not many witches survived the Wizard war, but those who did were hidden by common people who risked their own lives to protect them. In most creative ways, witches were hidden in secret compartments in houses, underneath the floor, inside or behind walls, anywhere were a small compartment could be built and sustain life for a limited time. Often these compartments were close to the main living area of the house, and the one in hiding had to keep very quiet during visits from other than the family who lived in the house and protected the secret. Of course, many were found or betrayed, dragged to the flames. Sometimes the angry mobs knew that they were not burning a witch, it could be that someone has uttered words against witch-burning in general, then you could be accused of hiding or sympathizing with the witches, and that was almost as bad as being a witch and definitely made you qualified to meet the creator in the purifying flames."

"The purifying flames?"

"Yes, it was said that a witch that was burned was forgiven the wrong-doings and would find peace in the afterlife."

"The afterlife?"

"Uhm, yeah, a belief that once you die, your body stays her in this world and decay, to give back to this world what was given to you from this world. While the soul, the true you, are traveling back to another world, a world that we cannot see with our eyes in this world. A world where our soul meets the creator and gets to be in the creator's paradise."

"Interesting. And you humans know this how?"

"Well, we don't know it as a fact, it's just a common belief."

"Huh, it is not far from the truth. Not the purifying the soul with flames part, but the soul, or energy, getting back to the origin in the multiverse."

"I will pretend I did not hear that and continue with something else. I think I have had enough of things I don't quite understand for one day!"

The Witch-hunt in reality

Roy's reflection is sadly accurate, when terrible things happens, it brings out both the best and the worst in people. Some act deliberately, some gets carried away, some just follows others. The human mind has a hard time coping with horrors. Like the mind short cuts.

Each time something terrible happens, there are a few opportunists that makes the terrible situation work in their advantage. A wise man once said it is the survival of the fittest, and in a way, it is applicable in this scenario as well. Only this time the enhanced ability is egoism rather than humanism.

An example that was present in every town, village and city. Accusing someone's husband or wife of being a witch to get the remaining part of the scattered marriage. Often as offered support and caring after the burning, only to swoop in take the empty place in the family, trying to make it whole again.

There are even examples of people accusing both their own partner and a partner of someone else, just to get another partner. Surprisingly often the plot succeeded in the advantage of the egoistic part.

A horrible side of the human species that I am sure that the creators did not intend. But then again, the creators cannot take responsibility for creatures that has been assigned free will. The power of free will is too great to anticipate the consequences of in forehand. Combined with other forces in the multiverse; choice, coincidence, luck, destiny, love, hope, faith, and many other forces that affects each and every human, the future of both the individual and the world and the entire multiverse is in an infinite state of change all the time.

The worst part of this witch-hunt, which makes it particularly bad, is that it was orchestrated to conceal the true aftermath of the wizard war. An aftermath I have not discovered the full extension of just yet. Without the orchestration, it might have been avoided completely and there would be one less wound to heal in this world.

The beauty of a world waking up according to Roy

"As a counterpoint to the horrors of the witch-hunt I need to fill my head with something beautiful again."

"Please do, dear friend, and please share it with me. I could also use something beautiful right about now."

"One of my favourite times of each day, especially here on the mountain, but also down there, in the world, among others, is the sunrise. As the night slowly slips away and let's go of everything, the stillness of everything still sleeping, starting with small sounds and small movements. The clear cold air is mixed up with warmer air. The tiny drops of dew glittering. The colours slowly changing in tone, getting brighter and brighter as the sun rises even further. Then at one point, almost like magic, it is no longer sunrise, nor morning, it is day. Everything has come back to its normal pace. The day is back in its normal routines and life is once again busy doing its thing. The state of rest has vanished, almost as if it has never existed."

"That is true beauty if anything…"

"And not only beautiful, but very fulfilling. I can get loaded with more energy those moments than I can get from one night's sleep."

"Has it always been like that? Even before you met Groll for the first time?"

"…I don't know, I was a different person back then and I don't think I ever took the time to enjoy the beauty of a world waking up…"

"I believe you… was just curious as if this loading with energy is something linked to the life essence. But I figure it can be other mechanisms in the human mind, or possibly the body, that can get that sensation…"

"I would definitely say that it is something others are capable of experiencing as well, not limited to me in any way."

"Ah, there we have it then."

"As I have been sitting here, doing a lot of thinking, I cannot help to think about the day and night as two different beings, guarding over everything, taking turns. But as day turns to night, the echoes of the day prevent our senses from experiencing the same thing at night. But it is possible, if you set your mind to it, and really let go of everything else, forcing yourself to be present in the moment. But in the morning, when you are rested, and you come from a different state of mind, it is much easier to take it all in. Your mind is not already crowded with everything going on around you, because things going on around you has not started just yet."

"Being present in the present, not distracted by the past, the possible future or anything else. Letting your emotions fill you, without controlling you. Being mindful without acting on every notion. That is something beautiful and something to try to achieve as often as possible."

"Not only at daybreak or at night?"

"No, it gives you greater power of your choices. Most humans are controlled by their emotions and let emotions have exclusive rights in guiding choices. And that is not wrong in any way, emotions are a good thing, given to you as guidance. But choice is one of the greatest powers in the multiverse, and when you let go of emotions, your mind can use the power of choice to accomplish great things."

"Are you saying that emotions make us make bad choices?"

"No, not at all, on the contrary. Emotions helps you make the best choices. Emotions are your guide. But emotion can also take you hostage and prevent you from making the best choice. But then again, any choice made actively is better than not to make a choice. An unmade choice, or passive choice, is a lost opportunity."

"Thus, a still and clear mind, reflecting on the choice at hand, the consequences of the choice, good and bad, for me and others, is the best choice?"

"Not necessary, the best choice is the one where you can live with the consequences, both foreseen and unforeseen. When you can live with your choice, regardless of other's opinions of your choice nor regrets of making it, then you have made the right choice. When an emotion holds you hostage, it is hard to make a choice that you will not question or regret later."

The beauty of a world waking up in reality

A world waking up and a world falling asleep is indeed beautiful things to witness. They are the same, but as Roy stated, it is easier to experience in the mornings, when the mind is less crowded and overwhelmed with impressions. But the mechanism is the same, day giving in to night, and night giving in to day. Like two wolves chasing each other. Sunrise and sunset being their tails. The day-wolf are full of energy and encourages activity. The night-wolf is a protector, encourages rest, fearless rest, the night-wolf will protect us. But not from each other, no, from other forces of the multiverse.

It is tricky to explain, given your current perspective and knowledge. So many things that you need to change to see it all, and to be able to grasp it all. I have no means to give you the full extent of it all. Besides, I am pretty sure that not even I have the full picture, nor that I will ever get it, no matter how hard I try to puzzle it all together. Simply too big and too many forces at work. Free choice only being one aspect of it all.

In the vacuum in between the two wolves, a fragile moment filled with expectations, possibilities and hope are formed by unexplainable forces in the multiverse. The human senses can barely perceive the vacuum but can grasp the silhouettes of it... and it is true beauty.

The cruel ruler according to Roy

"How about good choices and evil choices?"

"What do you mean?"

"Good and evil, perspective I guess?"

"Can you elaborate?"

"There once were a cruel ruler. He took prisoners, sometimes for no reason. These prisoners were kept in a special place and needed to fight for their freedom. Both against dangerous animals and each other. The fights were arranged in a big arena for everyone to watch. As entertainment. He sacrificed other people's life for the entertainment of himself and the people he ruled. And when his army conquered new territory he had the battles described in glorious words that described his own army and its achievements as powerful and invincible, while the losing party always were described as unworthy lowlifes who only got what they deserved."

"Well, the winner writes the history."

"But what about the truth, and good and bad?"

"As you said, perspectives. Think of it as everything you hear or read, everything you yourself communicate, is an opinion, a perspective, corrupted by senses and preconceptions."

"But I have a hard time to accept that there aren't true good and true bad in the multiverse."

"It is still always opinion and perspective."

"Simplify it for me."

"Your world, and your perspective is not different from this cruel ruler you just talked about."

"How can you say that?"

"Because it comes back to choice. And please keep in mind, everything I say has first been interpreted by my senses, filtered through my previous experience, my opinions, likes and dislikes, and then formed to words and all this before they even hit you, and go through the same process in you. And the cruel ruler also has the same filters, and from his point of view, he does what he thinks is the best, for himself and for those he rules. This is not defending him in any way, but he also makes choices. Same as you and me, but with totally different points of view, values, experiences, thoughts. Including his point of view of right and wrong."

"But isn't it wrong to kill? To destroy?"

"Is it?"

"Yes! Of course it is! Isn't it?"

"Is it wrong for an animal to kill another animal? Out of something that is destroyed, by human hands or otherwise, does it give something new a possibility?"

"Yes, but killing to eat is a totally different thing."

"Is it? In the long run, if I kill you, wouldn't it mean that I could get better possibilities to get food of my own, without your competition and without your mouth that also require food?"

"Maybe, but there is also the possibility that if you and I work together, we could accomplish even more."

"It is! And again, choice. Individually made. And when a certain number of individuals agree on the same choice it can be really powerful. But it is not a law in nature that everybody should agree, or that things are just. The world is created imperfect, the multiverse is imperfect, it has to be to give choice a place. Should everything be perfectly ordered there are no room for choice. No room whatsoever, then everybody and everything can only follow predetermined paths. And avoiding from the path would cause imbalance. So, the only way a perfect world and perfect order could exist is without free choice, and even then, it would not be perfect, it would be so fragile that it most likely would fall apart."

"But…"

The cruel ruler in reality

The cruel ruler did indeed make solid choices, choices that supported his vision of the future. A powerful nation with a strong history to guide it forward. Sacrificing a few along the way for a greater good was a price he was willing to pay. At first, he kept listing all of names of the people who died in his cause. He believed it was important to remember them, recognize their sacrifice, but he stopped doing that. Too many names, too many people affected by it. He eventually settled with giving them a day of their own. A day before each winter where everybody should remember and honour their dead. To most it became a celebration of the ones who walked before them, but for those who had a recent loss it was a day of mourning.

Like the Wizard, I will never defend the choices made by others, good or bad, because from another perspective, the choice always looks different. Like a coin with two sides, two persons can stand on different sides of the coin and argue on what they see. But in this I have to stress out that people often get stuck in arguing of what is on the opposite sides of the coin and forget about everything that connects those two sides, making it whole, complete. A coin is not just a motif on one side or the other. It does not only have two sides. It is a thing of its own, where the two different sides are just ways of seeing it. The sides do not define it in any way but is still a part of its whole. Equally apart of its whole. Equally true to describe the coin, but even the most detailed description of the one side, or even both sides, does not describe the whole coin. And to describe either side, both or the entire coin you have to use your perspective, your relation to the coin, and in doing so, you describe your relation and your perspective to the coin, rather than the coin itself. Very few people can objectively describe something. And even objectivity is affected by the own perspective.

The silver egg according to Roy

"You where there when they killed Rueen, weren't you?"

"Yes!"

"Hard to accept, isn't it?"

"Yes! And every time I think of it, I come to the conclusion that killing her is wrong, from any perspective!"

"Ah, but not to the black witches! Their perspective is to use the power of nature for their own good. Their perspective is that nature has denied them their full potential and it is their right to grab what is in reach and expand their natural limit beyond anything they can imagine."

"But they are wrong!"

"Yes, they are, from your perspective! And what says that your perspective is right. Even good? And the other perspective is bad and wrong? Now don't get me wrong, I do not defend their perspective in any way, and I agree with you, I also think it is wrong, even if I have a different perspective than you."

"And at the same time, I do not agree with Groll for creating the silver egg. I told him not to do it, but he would not listen. He thought it would be safest for everybody to bury it and hide it from everyone, guarded by the werewolves. But I thought it was an accident waiting to happen. And I was right. Somehow, they got out, somehow the egg was stolen, keeping causing bad things."

"Groll, a good person, from your perspective, making a bad choice, from your perspective, but good from his perspective. His perspective: hiding the silver egg will prevent evil in this world. Your perspective: creating the silver egg will encourage and reinforce evil in this world. Am I close?"

"Pretty close!"

"Here's my view. Each choice made by any individual, has a good or bad intention. There is no way to determine the consequence of the choice before it is made. Any good intention cannot be validated in advance. There is only the choice, with a thought behind it. The choice leads to consequence. Regardless of intention and regardless of point of view, that is the mechanics behind every choice. And that is also the power of the choice. Adding your intentions and your perspective is a way for you to make the choice, it does not determine the outcome of the choice. And as others apply their intentions and their perspective on your choice, they see something totally different."

"You know what? I think I should stop calling you a Wizard and start calling you a Wiseard!"

The Wizard laughed out loud, so loud that the laughter echoed along the mountain walls.

"You are funny, Roy, I'll give you that!"

"This conversation complicates everything for me, but it also makes me realize a lot of things and strengthen some of my views and believes. Even justifies some of my actions that I have somewhat questioned before. It gives me a fresh start. And that is something I need and welcome as I am about to re-join the others."

The silver egg according to Roy

"You where there when they killed Rueen, weren't you?"

"Yes, and it was painful to see."

"Do you ever regret not being able to help her?"

"Wait, I have a strange feeling of déjà vu... Haven't we had a conversation almost like this one before?"

"No wonder, we just experienced a tiny time-wave..."

"What is that?"

"You know when you jump in time. That is a big time-wave moving you through time. This tiny wave only moved us a little bit, this time back in time, a minute or so..."

"Ok, strange, but I will pretend like it didn't happen. How do you know I was not able to help her?"

"I see everything, remember?"

"Vaguely, but fair enough.... Yes, it was painful to watch and often I have thought if I could have done something to save her."

"Cold you?"

"I always wish that the answer would be 'yes', but each time I come to the conclusion that I could not have saved her, and each attempt would most likely result in both of us getting killed."

"Sounds about right."

"It's a good thing that Groll and Rueen created the silver egg, else who knows how events had unfold after her death."

176

"This is one of few black spots on my map. The silver egg. What do you know about it?"

"I have never seen it up close, but Groll and Rueen told me only a few bits and pieces, kept most of it secret. Most I've learned from rumours over the ages."

"Start with what they told you."

"Well, they said that they had taken out and secured their greatest tool since some witches had turned against them. And that they had locked it away where no one would ever find it."

"Not much to go on…"

"No, not really. I learned that the whole witch situation had escalated right before they captured and killed her, had no idea about it before that. And after I have tried to protect it, whatever it was, and each time I heard something that could be a clue to where it was hidden, I tried to destroy it. Strangely enough, I was not alone in this mission. But I do not know who else was trying to cover it up. At first, I thought it was Groll, but shortly after Rueen died he disappeared, and I haven't seen him since."

"Must have been hard for you… all this…"

"What do you mean with all this?"

"Everything, your unnatural long life, jumping, falling through time, not being able to connect or belong…"

"Well, yes, in a way… but still I would not have wanted anything to be different, at least not for my part. Loosing Rueen and then Groll, yes, it was hard, but somehow, I figure that I never really lost him, it was only him who lost his way for a while. I mean, after all, he met me before he gave me the life essence. And since I am here, he never hesitated on giving it to me, and in a way let me be reborn…

so in a way, you and Groll are my two fathers in this life. Without you I would not be here or be who I am…"

"Happy little accidents..."

"Call it whatever you want, but I feel kind of blessed. As folks say, blessed by the creator… and indeed I have been, literally!"

"Hold on, the time-wave will pass us again, and from the looks of it, these past minutes will vanish."

The silver egg in reality

When Groll and Rueen extracted their life essence and hid it away in a closed cave, surrounded by werewolves, they expected it to be hidden for ever. Their only worry was that it might be found by the dwarves, but that was something they thought of after sealing off the cave. But by then it was too late. They hoped that the protective instinct of the werewolves would include the dwarves trying to take the egg. And if they tried, it would most likely mean the end of the dwarves.

Groll was right in his suspicion that it was Leola that broke the seal to the cave. But she quickly realized that she would not be able to get the egg out of there, and she managed to not be detected by the werewolves using magic.

But she did leave the cave open on purpose, in hopes that somebody else would find it and lure the werewolves out. Her plan was to go back and get the egg as the werewolves were unleashed out into the world.

But her plan failed miserably. Those unfortunate who entered the cave was curious travellers who tried to find shelter in bad weather… when they stumbled right into the werewolf nest, and woke them up, they fled without noticing the egg. All got slaughtered by the horde of werewolves that flowed like a river through the cave and outside. Once outside they smelled more humans nearby and speeded away to slaughter that threat as well. And before the pack returned to the cave, a search party found the little remains of the travellers and followed the traces back into the cave and found the egg. Of course, they brought it with them. That's how it fell into the hands of man.

And once Leola discovered werewolves out in the world, she immediately returned to the cave, only to find the egg gone and the empty cave guarded by a few werewolves. Yet again she managed to use her magic to stay undetected.

As for the time-wave part, I am not sure just on how to comment that, so I'll just leave it be... but from your perspective, since the last conversation never happened, although it did, I guess the first conversation is the one who continues below.

Founding a society according to Roy

"A changed perspective. Interesting what dialogue with others can do to you."

"Yes, and I also find it more impressive that people actually can come together and accomplish things as a part of a whole, rather than as individuals. Or at least that is what I used to think."

"What do you mean?"

"A society is more we than me. We can accomplish things together. We can make things better together. We can cooperate and be greater together. Far greater than the individual. But now a day, I believe that the people is more me than we. What can I gain while contributing as little as possible? That's how I started out. But now when I have seen all the hard work that built our society, I feel like I want to keep contributing with what I can, when I can. Not for my own gain but for the common good."

"You mean that if you combine your egoistic points of view and incorporate what is good for more than only you, you'll get more out of helping others to a greater goal?"

"No, I mean that despite the greater goal makes me as an individual loose more than I gain, it can still be worth contributing. Not always gaining and not always keeping my own perspective and my own best in mind, I can help build something greater than me, who will be beneficial for more people than me. Might not even be beneficial to me, but still worth committing to. I believe, don't know, even if I have lived for a very long time, that in the long run, it is most beneficial to all individuals. I believe when you help others, and genuinely want to help, you'll get it back somehow."

"But isn't it just another view of an egoistic perspective?"

"Maybe, but I see the egoistic perspective as instant gain, or semi instant gain. I do something for you, and I'll be rewarded straight away, or I do something for you, and you owe me one that I can cash in later. This is more like, I do something for you now, without wanting something in return and someday, maybe, somebody else does something for me, without expecting something in return."

"Pay it forward..."

"Come again?"

"Never mind, just a good movie. But what I mean is that you give something without expecting something in return, and still expect something in return at a later point by someone else."

"Yes and no. Yes, in the perspective that if everybody thinks like this, unselfish, I think we should expect something in return at some point. And no, in the perspective that most people end up giving more than they get, while only a small part of the population receives more than they contribute."

"Sounds unfair."

"Sounds like a society where everybody is needed and has something to contribute. Even little things matter. Not everybody needs to be a great constructor or the best hunter or baker or chef. Someone that needs a lot of support and help can still provide an important function. Everybody has a place in a society. Everybody has a purpose."

"Even somebody that is born without the ability to contribute?"

"What do you mean?"

"Physical dysfunctions, mentally challenged people, list can be made much longer..."

"Still has a place to fill. Even if you have physical dysfunctions, cannot speak or communicate, you are still capable of receive love, and give love."

"Ah, love, the greatest power in the multiverse, without question!"

Founding a society in reality

Roy has a unique perspective on this. Both the perspective over time, which in itself is very unique and hard to gain other than being Roy, but also the perspective of the change in point of view. From being born with a most egoistic relationship to everybody and everything. What can I gain here and now, what will it cost me, and can I get it for less? And then the transformation to a different perspective. What can I contribute with in this situation? Can I fulfil what I start and commit to it 'til it's done?

The total change in perspective during a lifetime is not uncommon, but not very common either. Most people stay within their own comfort zone and does not challenge the values taught to them as children. But to most people that changes perspective, the changes takes places in a set of events that are separate occasions but are linked together by tiny details. Those events can be close in time or spread over several years. In Roy's case, the changes have been unusually slow. People who change perspective does in within their lifetime, but for Roy it took several lifetimes (measured by other's life) to reach the perspectives he now possesses. And faith willing, he will be around to change his perspective several times more, perhaps equally slow.

However, regarding the commitment to society Roy is spot on the truth (argued that there in fact is something that can be called a truth). The society that blossoms are full of individuals that want to cornubite with more than the get in return. Also, aware that what they get in return, they had not been able to get on their own. Everybody has their own set of skills and every set is needed as part of the whole, to make the machinery complete and functional.

The vampire door according to Vladir

"Is it really?"

"The greatest power in the multiverse? Undoubtable! Love has everything, forgiveness, support, destruction, affection, attachment, beauty, patience... the list is long..."

"But is love really a single thing, isn't it endless variations of different things?"

"What do you mean?"

"Take Vladir, he is a skilled woodcraftsman. His love for wood and carving has allowed him to create the most beautiful things. Like the doors to the Vampire master's main hall, like the throne he made for grand master Phidas, like... well, another long list of beautiful objects... but that love, is that the same force that connects him with Yena? I mean, isn't than a whole other thing all together?"

"Yes, and no... as always..."

"Again, perspective?"

"No, for once it's not perspective..."

"Elaborate..."

"You know matter, the thing that makes up every physical thing around you, and even you..."

"Stones, wood, water, air?"

"Yes, matter is in a way energy, only in a different state. Or, at least you see it as different state. The matter in you and in the mountain are not different. And the matter in a living being is not different from that of a dead being. The difference would be the soul. Now

185

the soul, that is also energy… and to simply it, the difference between those energies are their frequency, or wavelength."

"Wavelength?"

"Think of it as waves on the oceans, sometimes the ocean is calm without waves, sometimes it is only tiny ripples on the surface, where the top of each tiny wave is close to each other. And sometimes there are wave on a roaring sea, where the top of each wave is far from each other. This is wavelength. The closer the tops, the shorter the wavelength. The longer apart the tops are, the longer the wavelength is. It is called frequency."

"Ok, so matter is the same only different frequency's, and the soul is also matter, but in another frequency?"

"Something like that…"

"And love?"

"Love would be how these different frequencies come together, how they build harmonies…"

"Harmonies?"

"Take the doors to the vampire masters main hall, the one's that Vladir carved. His love for wood carving makes him in harmony with the wood, but it is not only the wood, it is also the various tools he is using, where he is when he carves, what lightning there currently is, what other things that are around him at the moment of creation… plenty of frequencies that coexists and meet at a certain point in time. Should it reach harmony, the frequencies will work together and the thing that forms in the spaces in between is love. The thing binding it all together."

"So, love the human feeling and love the multiversal force is two different things?"

"Yes and no, love the human feeling is the human interpretation of the multiversal force…"

The vampire door in reality

The love that resonated when Vladir created the doors for his (at the time) master was beautiful and detailed. Although I have never seen them, Vladir can describe them into tiniest detail and have as painting words as he has carving hands.

Each and every important event in the vampire history is recorded on those doors, from the moment of creation through the uprising against the Wizards and Witches, every major battle (in the Wizard war in particular) and political victories such as the trade agreement with the dwarves and the acquisition of their strong hold. The blank spot on the lower right door was saved for the final chapters but since Vladir escaped from the vampire clan, there were no one to finish the work, and it would stay untouched until that moment when Vladir reunited with the doors after uncountable time apart.

That was not something Vladir was aware of when he was about to start the destruction of the sky road, and frankly never could expect since the castle was blown into rocks and dust by Phidas and Roy. But the future, from their current perspective, carried many surprises to all of them, not only to Vladir and the beautiful doors, but to all of them, Roy, Phidas, Veron, heck, the entire dwarf society for that matter, and to Dee, Rick and Tadao, all of them awaited futures that neither of them could imagine.

The legendary beggars according to Roy

"Again, perspective I guess?"

"As always, dear Roy!"

"I have a question for you, since you seem to know just about everything about, well everything…"

"I will answer it if I see it fit to do so!"

"I guess there is no secrets behind my question, but it is regarding the beggars, and not any beggars, specifically two beggars, Ben and Luke."

"What about them?"

"I met them once, going south to restart… as always, they travelled together. They mistook me for one of their traits since I was travelling alone. And when I tried to convince them of not being one of them, we got flooded by a horde undead. Naturally, I have encountered them many times, even if it was not that many, and I knew just about how to avoid them, as did the beggars. Only they had a different tactics. That situation did not help me convince them, since it's not very common to be able to avoid undead other than fighting them, which would be impossible in that situation, due to their great numbers."

"Ah, yes, I remember, I've watched the three of you during that situation several times… quite the handywork you all did!"

"Seen it several times? Never mind, I have a feeling that's another thing I will have hard to wrap my head around. Anyway, during our manoeuvres, or rather, *their* manoeuvres, I could not help but to wonder if they master some kind of magic. Even if what I saw did not come close to any witch or wizard I have ever seen, yet they did some astonishing work that I cannot explain in any other ways than magic."

"I will answer this in two ways. Perhaps one of the two answers will satisfy your curiosity."

"Is both answers the truth?"

"Yes, and as always, perspectives."

"Figures, but get to it, I am curious!"

"From your perspective, you have travelled backwards in time, to a place much earlier in the timeline of this world. In doing so, you have brought knowledge from the future to the past, and had you chosen to use and apply some of your future knowledge, it might have appeared like magic to those who watched you that are native to the past. Not because you use magic, but because you do things that they have no reference to, or experience to relate to what they see, so they are unable to process the things they see and are limited by their own understanding of the world. Overtime, taking small steps in a slow pace, as knowledge grows, new reference points form for the general population, and it is looked upon as progress and development rather than magic. And remember, you asked about these two beggars in particular, not beggars in general."

"So, what you are saying is that they are from a future of this world?"

"No, that is only one of the answers. The other answer would be, interestingly enough just after we have already discussed something similar... Love, frequencies and harmonization. Do you know the vegetable onion?"

"Onion? Yes, why?"

"Then you know that the onion is composed of several thin layers, some of those thin layers are combined to a thicker layer, yet each thicker layer is composed of several smaller layers. Are you following so far?"

"Yes, so far, but I have a feeling that this is possibly the last point in this part of this conversation that I can say that I understand."

"Okey, I'll try to walk you through it. With layers in an onion, they exist inside and outside each other, not occupying the same space at the same time, because that would be impossible, right?"

"So far, yes, I still follow."

"As I have said earlier, time and space does not really exist, it is only perception."

"Perspective?"

"Yes, in a way. Now think about the layers of the onion. Then imagine that each layer is a separate world, but unlike the onion they are not lined up and stacked on each other, they occupy the same space."

"How is that possible?"

"Different frequencies. As there are different space in this universe, there are different space, at the same place in the multiverse."

"Yup, lost me…"

"I'll continue, see if you catch on eventually… some layers of the multiverse share the same space in the multiverse, or rather, is the same space, same matter, only different frequencies of it. And that's were perspective comes in once again. The perspectives being time, space and layer of space. Three dimensions of the same matter. But not the three dimensions you see when you talk about matter, you say width depth and height, that is your three dimensions. They are also three true dimensions, but not the same as these three other dimensions."

"No, still lost…"

"Ah, in time you might get it, but for now, with that background, Ben and Luke are manipulating the layers of space in the multiverse, phasing in and out. But they are not so skilled that they can leave this world and pass through to another, they only change their frequencies enough to slip a little out of this world, making them both here and not here. The not here part is what saves them from being injured, and the here part allows them to still move around here, navigating their surroundings."

"Gotcha, being here and not here at the same time, kind of makes sense. How does time fit in this picture?"

"It doesn't, but phasing in and out of this world allowed them to detect and avoid the timewaves in this layer of this world. But they only learned that after their first encounter with a timewave."

"That put them back in time?"

"That put them here, out of their own time."

The legendary beggars in reality

*Ben and Luke got pushed through time in a timewave, and they
tried several times to get back to their own time, but always failed
miserably, and seem to get to a worse period in time for each wave
they passed. When they got to a reasonable time, they decided to
stay, even if they did not like it particularly much. But they had seen
worse. Now, they did not have the luxury of immortality as Roy did,
but their knowledge of the layers and different frequencies
protected them to some extent from the decay of time that happen to
most people.*

*They would cross ways with Roy once more, to Roy's advantage,
but to their disadvantage, if you count being alive as an advantage.
From their perspective, they did not mind leaving it all behind,
purifying their energy and phases to be one with the multiverse.
Their aid much needed to Roy and his companions at the time. And
a relief for Ben and Luke.*

Kidnapping the dwarf king according to Roy

"Putting them out of their own time. Now I cannot help but to think that they do not have the same advantage as me, I have seen them age."

"Yes, you could say that they got kidnapped by time itself, hold hostage without the possibility to be released or to pay ransom."

"You know, that reminds me, do you know what made Phidas ally with the vampires?"

"No, I cannot say that I have looked into that, of course, I can do it, but if you'd like to tell me, it would be much better and a far greater pleasure!"

"As you know, dwarves get ridiculously old."

"Look who's talking."

"I know, but I feel there is a difference between naturally old age and enhanced old age. Those who'll get old as they were created has a much better chance of coping with it well, rather than me who have had my ups and downs over the ages, these last years would count as a down…"

"Have you had other downs?"

"Oh, yes! Several…"

"Tell me about one… and how did it matter?"

"Most of my downs have probably not mattered, I have only been absent. But once, and this is something I assume I will answer to in a nearby future, I had a chance to intervein in a historical event, that could have had a potentially large change of the events that followed. Maybe even impact the events of this entire world."

"You do have a skill of talking a lot without saying anything, only to build curiosity, you know that?"

"Old habit, I guess. I rather enjoy telling stories and keep my audience's attention on me..."

"And my undivided attention you have! Please continue!"

"When I joined Phidas on his mission to destroy the vampires, I did not know that I could have stopped his misery long before he made the choice that he later regretted."

"Still building up to it, aren't you?"

"Yeah, you'll just have to patiently wait for it... like everybody else who listens to me and my stories."

"Patiently waiting then, without more interruptions, I'll guess you'll get faster through the build-up and to the core of the story faster if I talk less..."

"Well, you know Phidas regretted that he traded the tiny piece of life essence to the vampire master?"

"Yes, I know that... and now I believe you are stalling more by getting me to talk more..."

"Haha, perhaps... sorry, I'll get to it... the reason for his decision was not only dwarf greed. During the wizard war, the vampires managed to capture Sephidas, Phidas' grandfather. Phidas was one of few who knew this. He never shared this with others, since he was not entirely sure that his father, Midas, was not involved in this somehow, to gain access to the throne. Either way, apart from enormous wealth in gemstones and valuable metals, various art artefacts and a peace treaty between dwarves and vampires, he also got the release of his grandfather, Sephidas. But it backfired, Sephidas had grown both old and demented and did no longer identify as a dwarf. He believed he was one of the vampires and chose to stay among the vampires once his freedom was given to him. But Phidas got several of his grandfather's journals and other personal items from the time in captivity, things his grandfather did no longer consider his own. The price for all that Phidas gained was just the tiny piece of life essence, nothing more."

Kidnapping the dwarf king in reality

The truth behind it all, was that the vampires did kidnap King Sephidas and held him in captivity for the duration of his long life, and it was a greedy and power-hungry conspiracy behind the kidnapping. The payment from Midas to the vampires was in large everything that Phidas got back for the life essence. And it was King Midas who was the brain behind it all. Unfortunately, he died at the end of the wizard wars, and Phidas took his place in the main mines, as Grand Master, since he still saw his grandfather as the true King, conspiracy or not.

And since Sephidas figured the whole thing out, he turned his back on the dwarf society and the dwarf way of life, hurt and disappointed of the betrayal. And when he got the chance to return, he only played demented to get out of having to return. During his stay with the vampires, even if held captive, he grew quite close to the lot of them, and the feelings were mutual. Sephidas challenged the most intellectual vampires and got challenged by them. One vampire in particular had a special bound to the prisoner, endlessly discussing art among other things, and yes, you have probably guessed it... Vladir. The two had great exchange of ideas, discussion of art, of life... Thus, when Sephidas passed away of old age, Vladir had lost the one reason to stay in the vampire stronghold. It was time for him to leave, and shortly, he met Roy, and even if one friendship cannot fill the void of another, the friendship with Roy filled Vladir with renewed hope and joy.

How Phidas got the life essence in the first place according to Roy

"Do you know how Phidas got hold of the life essence?"

"No, that is a piece of information I have never come across…"

"Do you like me to share? I mean, you have given me a great deal today, figure I could give you a story in return."

"Oh, I'd like that very much! And I do not think it classifies as any information I can have to get leverage in anything anymore."

"There is no such information! All pieces of information can always be used to gain leverage in something at some point. Even if the information is outdated."

"I'll keep that in mind!"

"Anyway, the life essence was brought to him as the most valuable finding of the first day in a new mining expedition. Customary for all new mining expeditions to bring forth the most valuable finding of the first days mining to the dwarf master."

"As a reward or a bribe?"

"I believe as gratitude, it is the dwarf master that approves all new mining operations and it is either a private funded mining operation, a clan funded or funded by the dwarf master for the dwarf society."

"Ah, so the dwarves aren't just mining every day, for the prospect of finding something that the mountain has not yet revealed?"

"In a way, but everything costs, and mining benefits only those who are willing to pay the price. And each mining expedition is a risk, since there is not a guarantee what will come out of it. In fact, most mining operations costs more than it gains. Now a days that is."

"You said that the life essence was the most valuable object found on the first day, how do they know what is the most valuable?"

"Well, the crown always appoints a master treasurist. It is the duty of the treasurist to value every object that is found. And record it in the books for the mining operation. Each finding must be noted to be legit, and only legit objects can later be traded."

"A little lesson in dwarf society, that can always come in handy!"

"Oh, you do not know how right you are, or what their history contains… you would be amazed how much there is to tell about the dwarves!"

"I am sure! And to be frank, it wasn't much of information as to Phidas got the life essence, a finding, brought to the Grand master as customary. No fancy tail at all."

"I am sorry for it not being very colourful, but not all truthful stories are…"

"Ah, come on, every dull truthful story can be spiced up by adding a little colour. It is not difficult."

"Can you give me an example?"

How Phidas got the life essence in the first place in reality

Roy was right, there is always the possibility to add colour to any story, but in this case, it was not needed, but the Wizard failed to mention the colourful bits of this story.

One of the colours would be the fact that this was a privately funded mining expedition, and as such it was not very uncommon that the individual who funded the mining expedition, and the appointed treasurist, most anyway, would keep some items off the books. Most often, the most valuable. Tradition states that the funder keeps the most valuable, the treasurist the second most valuable, and the third most valuable object was given to the Grand Master and also happened to be the first object appearing in the books. Black market objects were a very lucrative business for many dwarves.

But the most interesting part is not that the life essence was being found and wrongfully valued by the treasurist. The most interesting part is how it got there in the first place.

The life essence originated from Rueen, as a gift to one of the most powerful wizards of the human race, Ora. You'll probably hear more about here, if you are following the events of this world. Ora was curious about the power of the life essence and Rueen was kind enough to get her a tiny piece. The problem with a tiny piece of life essence is that it contains far more power and energy than anybody can imagine. Of course, Rueen knew this, but trusted Ora with it.
Ora on the other hand, she realised how much power that was contained in that tiny piece and she quickly understood how this much power could be misused in the wrong hands.

That insight made her act irrational, and she took it to the mountain, using her powerful magic to bury the tiny piece deep into the solid rock, where she was certain that it would never be found.

Later, she thought it would have been better to give it back to Rueen, but by then she had forgotten exactly where she had buried it.

An example of adding colour to a story according to Roy

"Ok, an example… what do you know about rainbows?"

"Rainbows?"

"Yes, Rainbows. Colourful things that appear after rain or in misty areas when sunlight comes…"

"Ah, yes, well I know just about what you just said. Maybe also that they can appear beneath waterfalls, if the sunlight hits it right…"

"Yes, and from my experience, there is not much to them. You cannot touch them, they have no beginning, no end. They cease to exist if you remove the sunlight or the mist."

"I've seen one as a circle once… a complete circle, not only a bow."

"This supports my theory even further. Now how to spice this up, no need to add colour I mean…"

"Hahaha, good one, dear Roy! Good one!"

"First thing. No one can touch a rainbow. Secondly. A rainbow almost always appears at a distance, and when you move, it looks like it moves to. So, when you get to the place you thought the rainbow were, it still appears in the distance. Or it's gone."

"Yeah, sounds about right so far."

"Now, what if we make up something to add to the rainbow, something mystical. Like a treasure in the end of the rainbow, just where it touches ground."

"A treasure, like a pot of gold?"

"Yes, either that or a pot of gemstones for the dwarves, or a basket of food for the hungry. A deliberate lie, that cannot be checked nor proven wrong, and with the sole purpose of entertaining the imagination. Not doing any harm, just broaden perspective, challenge the imagination and expanding the individual's thoughts to something new."

"I see that, but what is the point of colouring the story?"

"To make it more interesting, and to expand our way of thinking. If we are to use our imagination to solve problems, then our imagination needs to be challenged and trained in to thinking outside of our daily boundaries."

"Ok, give me another example."

Another example of adding colour to a story according to Roy

"Say walking in a forest in the mist. Would you consider it dangerous or safe?"

"Well, for humans and most other species native to this world, dangerous of course."

"Why is it dangerous?"

"Well, werewolves, vampires and undead for one, hungry animals for two, and a bunch of other stuff that I am sure you know I know for three."

"And would you want to tell a child about all the horrible things in the forest?"

"Not if I wanted it to walk in the forest, no."

"Then what if you told a child that there are dangerous things in the forest, but also marvellous thing. Creatures that are possible to encounter only in mist or in darkness?"

"Would they believe such a thing?"

"Yes, and they would be very alert when in the forest in the dark or in the mist, trying to grasp anything that could be related to the mythical creature."

"Ah, and an alert child would also discover dangers…"

"Exactly… again, a deliberate lie to challenge and expanding the imagination to be used for something more and beyond the daily borders."

"What would such a mythical creature be?"

"Uhm, it could be… a… uhm… a Unicorn!"

"And what is a Unicorn?"

"It's a white horse with silver mane, and a horn in the forehead, just one in the middle above the eyes, pure white. And it would have magical powers. If you come close enough to touch the horn, it can grant you a single wish."

"And children believe this?"

"Turns out that some parents believe it too…"

"So, that is why over half the people of this world believes in unicorns, because you made them up!"

"Yes, I suppose. But I did not intend for it to be anything else other than a story for the kids."

"I see, and Unicorns does not have anything in common with rainbows?"

"No, but at first I was about to say that their poop would have the colours of the rainbow, but I quickly dismissed that idea, since no one would ever find rainbow coloured poop in the woods."

"Smart move, young man. That is what I hate about things that are made up. There is always a chance that you tangle yourself in it, and it will not be pretty when the lie is exposed. Never is."

"No, never. That is why I always try to only colour stories, not make stories up. Colouring can add value, lies cannot."

"I can agree to that…"

"But what about all those who claims to have seen a Unicorn?"

"Well, I guess their imagination got the better of them."

"Huh, so it has nothing to do with that I have created one and implanted it on this world?"

"You have?"

"Yes, hidden in time and space, just like the house, but also hidden in mist or the dark…"

"Like a white horse? With a horn?"

"Yes!"

"Does it grant you a wish if you touch the horn?"

"Yes, as per reputation. Only one thing… it is almost impossible to get close to it…"

"Why is that?"

"How would it look like if everybody could get their wishes granted?"

"Probably crazy. And for the best that it is almost impossible to get close to it… but just out of curiosity, can you get close to it?"

"Yes, you can. But you have to walk slowly to it, both hands raised over your head showing it your empty hands. And if it senses someone else nearby, it will run away. But alone and approach it slowly, it is possible. And as a last safeguard, when you get about 30 feet from it, it will charge against you with the head bent down, horn ready to stab you. But if you stand still and wait for it to come, it will stop right in front of you, without harming you, and let you touch its horn."

"Huh, I guess most people would start to run away from it when it charges against them."

"I am counting on it."

Adding colour to a story in reality

These thoughts Roy shared with the Wizard on the mountainside, they were pretty recent insights. Even so, Roy had added colour to his stories for as long as he could remember, without knowing why, or without knowing there were different kinds of lies. Roy had a natural talent for either exaggerate a perspective to absurdity or adding a balanced amount of colour without pushing it to a complete lie and without risk being accused of lying. Well, mostly anyway. On occasion Roy has been caught with lies, and it has always ended bad when he has been caught. For some reason it is always the wrong people who see through a lie. People who often have things to hide themselves. A lie towards them means that you are a liability, and could possibly threaten their own integrity, their own need for keeping their facade. Well, this is mostly me rambling and speculating, perhaps from my own experience. And I am the first to confess that my experience hardly is speaking for everybody. Anyway, let's continue this book, shall we?

Oh, before I forget. The Unicorn. I have seen it. And I have tried following the secrets revealed to me by the Wizard. It worked, and I got my wish granted. What did I wish for? A story for another time. But for now, rest assure that it is real and that it in fact grants your wish, whatever it may be.

Eating according to Roy

"I have to confess, I have lost track of time. I've been sitting here for so long that I even have lost track of how many times I have lost track of time and have tried to figure out the time again. You wouldn't happen to know how much longer it is before I vanish in my first time-wave-jump?"

"No worries, dear friend. I will leave here for my goodbye, and then you can wait a little while longer before you leave to re-join where you left…"

"Thank you! It is odd, one thing. Or many things really, but this one. Time has passed since I sat down on this spot. And for the first time in a very long time, I have not been a part of it, since I have already lived it. But not with the perspective I carry now. So, these years will always be a gap in my knowledge and memory. But as for the many ages I have walked this world, there are not many gaps, I have lived through it all."

"What would you say have changed?"

"Oh, a lot of things, far more things than I think we have time to cover here. But one of the small things, that has changed slowly is eating."

"What do you mean?"

"Well, take the first humans that Rueen and Groll created after the flood. They were created to this world, in my image, but there were no society surrounding them. They had to learn it all from scratch. Build everything from zero. I wasn't around to show them what to do and what not to do. And when I first encountered them, they were tiny and malnourished. Short in length. They fed of what they could find and gather. Berries, nuts, mushroom and so on. To get food their tribe needed to split up and move to different territories to get food to everybody. Those who stayed behind in their first area, they did not face any new challenges and did not develop much. As for the others, they adapted to their new environment and developed at far greater speed. While the first part of the tribe continued to eat poorly, others found other things to eat that gave them more nutrition, some started hunting, some started growing plants and the culture developed in various stages over the ages. The more nourishment the people got, the taller and more athletic they became, more and more like me, and the greater their capacity to survive and gather and capture food became. All the while, the first group stagnated, short and tiny. And food had grown from eating almost too little to keep the body functioning to have sustainable food, to have good food, to have food in abundance. And only the latter created fat people. It was practically unheard of before."

"I can see how this has affected people differently over time. What happened to the little people?"

"I am not certain. But sadly, I believe that they later were captured and held as slaves by those who had superior length and strength."

"The first slaves thus were the descendant of the first people. Ironic in a way!"

"Very ironic. And sad. I believe that they all died out in slavery, they just vanished over a relatively short period of time. And no one ever talked about them, seemed like no one cared."

"But I'd say that is quite common, not to care for slaves, no?"

"Maybe for most people, but for slavers, no, they care deeply over their investments and the capacity of their slaves. Almost as greedy as the dwarves."

"Some reason for caring…"

"But still, and not even among slavers where they talked about."

Eating in reality

The first tribe of the humans, short and thin as they were, they stayed together, kept true to each other. In their native area, they gathered what little food there were and shared among each other. They even learned how to grow certain types of mushrooms and other plants. That knowledge they brought with them in captivity and managed to develop to the harsh environment in dark cages with very little resources to cultivate and grow food. Nevertheless, this knowledge was the one thing that kept them alive after their time in captivity. And yes, they have a very interesting story to tell after their time in captivity, but that is noting I will share now, but I am certain that if you have followed this world so far, and continue to follow it, you will get your curiosity satisfied at some point in the future.

And the reflection Roy did, about having shortage of food in the beginning of humanity, splitting up to find more food and finding food richer in energy was a critical development for the survival of the people of this world. Without it, there would not be any fat people today who could live and prosper in abundance while others still starve on the brink of existence, clinging on to life itself. The overflow of energy in the food was at several points in history the only thing that kept the humans alive. With food shortage those on the brink died while those who had more survived, carried the humanity onward through history. War, diseases, epidemics and natural disasters have always had its toll on all life of this world. And even how unfair it seems, it has been for the greater good of humanity that some has survived those crises. Maybe not fair, but on the other hand, when is life completely fair?

Hard not to get to close according to Roy

"Speaking of caring... I keep wondering. About the ones getting close to you, and what it feels like to leave them behind. I cannot help but feeling that this must affect you greatly?"

"Of course, it does. The only person, other than Groll and Rueen, I have really connected with on a deeper level, so far, is Vladir. Even if his life, like my own, have a theoretical limit and we both can die, we haven't done that just yet. And have no plans of doing so in the near future... or ever, if we have any say in it... And I plan to hook up with Dee and Rick, they too would be immortal from their encounter with the life essence and Groll."

"Yes, they are... but you must have met other people throughout your lifespan?"

"Plenty, but I have managed to keep most at bay. Some have come closer and I have mourned them, mostly in the beginning..."

"Tell me about them, would you?"

"No, still too painful, even if it was ages ago."

"Then let me ask you this. If you do not talk about it, how do you ever expect the pain to go away?"

"Don't know. But I know that it has not worked so far."

"My point exactly."

"So, talk about it then, to who?"

"Well, me for one. And if you expect to get close to others, them to..."

"Others like who?"

"Well, I do not have to be a Wizard, nor have all my gifts, to see that your heart is yarning for someone in particular. "

"Like who?"

"You know, I know, and I would be very surprised if she does not know in a while, rather sooner than later…"

"Ok, so what has that to do with anything?"

"Well, if you start by telling me, you have opened the lid and released the hardest pressure. This way, when you tell her, it will not be as painful for you…"

"Oh, alright…"

"Alright what?"

"I'll tell you, just give me a moment."

Both sat quiet before Roy continued.

"I once was married. We had a child. Our child died young in a plague. I watch her grow old, and she watched me not age at all. Of course, she knew, I had to tell her. But when I buried her next to our daughter, I swore never to let anyone get close again."

"Good, you are staring to let it out! How did it feel?"

"Witch part?"

"All of it, first falling in love, then getting a child, the whole marriage, losing your child, watching the woman you love age and eventually die…"

"Painful…"

"Was all of it painful?"

"No, but the pain is kind of overshadowing the rest."

"Because you let it… you have to release the pain, get it out of your system, as you've started now. Below the cloud of pain is all the love and wonderful memories that you have had together with your family, use the strength of those memories to chase away the cloud of pain. No matter how strong the pain is, there are far greater power in the love!"

"It's strange, I've heard over the ages that time heals all wounds. I find it very untrue. All this time and it still hurts…"

"But it's true what they say. Time is also very powerful in healing, if you let it. You have closed it all inside you, locked it up and thrown away the key. In there, nothing can touch it and it will stay just the way it was when you locked it away. Let it out Roy! Let it crack open!"

"Strange, I've had almost infinite time up until now, and now when I am making ready to move on, I suddenly wish I had more time on my hands…"

Hard not to get to close in reality

*Time does heal all wounds, it is true, but you have to let it, and up
to that point, Roy had not let anything get to those memories. He
had closed them up in a cocoon inside of him. But normally,
cocoons are closed, stay closed for some time, then open up to
release a creature of beauty. Roy's inner cocoon had only hardened
over the ages and didn't seem to be ready to open up any time soon.*

*Being a husband was the second happies part of Roy's long life and
being a father by far the happiest. And at the time he had not
thought it through, just got caught up in it. But as his child died in
his arms, he realised that he never again should reproduce. The
horror of losing your child and not being able to follow your
grandchildren or their children. A curse to never die and always
outlive everybody you hold dear. Except perhaps Dee. What if he
got children with her? Another immortal human. But was she even
interested in him?*

*Time would give Roy the answer, time would also test his friendship
with Vladir. Time would both bless and curse Roy, as an immortal.
But before time could do either, he had to let go of the past,
reconcile with it, embrace it, all of it. Stop running from it. Let it
sink in, let it go, let it be.*

Time that counts according to Roy

"Well, no matter how much time you've already had, nor how much time you will experience, the interesting part about time is that you can never use any other time than the present."

"What do you mean?"

"Take a moment to think of what you've been doing here the past, well, almost for a lifetime…"

"I've been sitting here waiting for the right moment to continue with my life, while minimizing the chance of running into myself."

"Yes, both things are true, but you have also just let time pass…"

"As in I have not utilized it?"

"Exactly, time is almost like money, you need to spend it to make use of it, but unlike money, you cannot save it and use it later."

"What you are saying is that unless I use the time I have now, this moment, it is just wasted time?"

"Yes, now is all you've got to do anything. You cannot expect to do anything in the future, nor can you change anything you've done in the past."

"And to complicate it, time is one factor, choice is another…"

"Yes, and will would be a third, and there is a bunch of other perspectives that is part of now…"

"Does all this have a name that includes every perspective?"

"Almost… the closest would be reality… but even reality is a perspective…"

"So, basically there is no way for me to grasp everything ever?"

"Yes, and no… There is a built-in limitation of the human mind. That limitation restricts the thoughts, and your thoughts are the foundation of your language and words, and ironically the language are also a barrier for your thoughts and way to express yourselves."

"Again, I need to pretend that I understood that. But eventually I'll guess it will sink in and make sense."

"Probably… and to connect back to the initial question, present. It is truly a present. See what I did there?"

"No pun intended?"

"Oh, on the contrary, pun very intended!"

"You are quite something, aren't you?"

"In the eye of the beholder."

"Then you are! I am currently the beholder of you, and I say you are quite something!"

"Well, thank you, I'll take that as a compliment!"

"You should! I meant it as such."

Time that counts in reality

Pun or no pun, the present is really a present. Now is the only time that counts. Later may or may not exist. The past is unchangeable, for most anyway. Perhaps not for accidental time travellers as Roy or the Wizard, but for most it is very unchangeable."

This all means that each moment, each now that you experience, will ultimately shape your future. Weather you actively choose it or let whatever is coming come your way.

Like crossroads, you can always choose to keep going forward, never take a right (or wrong) or choosing left. Then what's left is not right but it will be straight ahead. And how interesting is it to always go straight ahead? Never knowing what you are missing around the corner.

Then again, the downside of a choice is that you will never know what the other options were since the options are always linked to a now. Exclusively existing only once. Each moment, a onetime offer, never to return, never to be undone. The upside being all events and opportunities that unfold.

And, not to forget. As the Wizard points out a little later, there are infinite perspectives on perspectives and the same goes for time and choice when it comes to unfolding events and opportunities. Opportunities that has passed will not return, but you might end up on the same road even if you make different choices. All choices do not always have their own paths, different choices can lead to the same path or the same place or the same persons, with the only differences is the heading and direction. Because that can also affect your views. Seeing the same thing from a different angel may very well result in a unique perspective.

The craziest thing according to Roy

"I'd like us to lighten the mood a bit, we have been very deep and serious for a while, and I'd like to move on with something a little lighter before it is time for me to get going."

"Do you have anything particular in mind?"

"No, but let's say… Let me see… What is the craziest thing you've ever done?"
"Oh, hard to say… Crazy like goofy, or immortal limit-pushing, or just humanly crazy as in not knowing why I did something?"

"Do I have to choose? I mean, often we are presented with options and can only choose one, but this time, can I choose all?"

"I guess… let's see, goofiest thing. Ought to be when I was a child, just before I lost my parents. It was autumn, I wanted so badly to have some sweets, but we could not afford it, so I dressed up in one of my mother's dresses and painted myself black in the face with aches from the fireplace. Then I walked to the nicer houses, knocked on their door and asked for a treat, threatened them with a trick if I didn't get a treat. Most people only laughed and closed the door in my face. So, I decided to wait until it was dark. Then most people were scared, and I got plenty of sweets. I must have looked awful, all black and smeared in the face and mother's way too big dress all around me."

"Sounds goofy enough!"

"But the goofiest part is that some other kids mimicked it the following autumn. Dressed up to scary creatures and went door-knocking. Became somewhat a tradition last day of the harvesting period. I never did it again. Lost my mother and father that winter, was left to tend for myself. My childhood was cut short. Learned to cheat and hustle on a bigger scale than knocking doors for treat. Got pretty good at it!"

"What about 'immortal limit-pushing' then?"

"Well, besides from sitting here? Because this is probably the most limit-pushing thing, not counting first time I tried going under water without being able to breath air, or living inside a giant sea creature or recovering from every injury or sickness?"

"Sounds like a lot of limit-pushing, and from a human perspective, that ought to be crazy stuff…"

"Then it leaves humanly crazy… which includes every act that Johari would put in the fourth square. I do not know why I am doing it and you do not know why I am doing it. For me it has always been emotional reactions. Overwhelming emotions. Like marrying my wife. Should I have reasoned with myself about the best course of action I would not have married at all, given my immortality. But as soon as I met her, I stopped thinking logically and my strong emotions for her drove me to one of the best decisions of my entire life, marrying her, even if we just had met."

"Good, you keep talking about her!"

"Way out of my comfort zone, but I could not think of any better person to talk to about her."

"I'm glad! And I value our bound. It has enriched my life very much, and I know it will yours as well."

"If you say so, I have a feeling you know far more than you say you do, and I would not be surprised if you intentionally set seeds here and there, only to watch them grow over time."

"You are a quick study, pick things up in a fast pace. Have easy to read between the lines, and it is often said more between the lines than the words that are used…"

The craziest thing in reality

Oh, so much pain dear Roy carried around. A completely different person back then, but that Roy would go through so much transformation. Heal his hurts. Embrace himself and his new life. All that in time. All that in good company. But he would suffer more losses, but when doing so, be better equipped to handle them.

The Wizard, of course, knew all this and did indeed plant a few seeds here and there, only to watch them grow over time. In fact, the Wizard planted so many seeds that if they were actual seeds, you would not see Roy, you would see a strange moving and talking forest, complete with trees, bushes, flowers, fungus', animal life, insects, heck, an entire ecosystem with its own flora and fauna.

And the craziest thing was in reality none of the things Roy did, but the motif the Wizard had. But as many times before, this is not the time and place for that story.

Learning everything according to Roy

"Yeah, but even if I am a quick study and read between the lines, I have not succeeded in my mission of learning everything!"

"What do you mean?"

"After I realized that I had travelled back in time and had settled in that, accepted my faith if you will, I started about thinking of things I could do with all this time. One of the first thing I figured I should do was to learn everything about everything and use that for personal gain and get wealthy. And in the beginning, I had the leverage. I knew some things that was not known yet. Not a great many things, but enough. And back then the general knowledge level was very low, and I pretty much grasped it all. But as knowledge develops some gets obsolete and new takes its place. All the while the total knowledge slowly grows. And even if some knowledge are forgotten and becomes a part of the past, there is simply no way, for me at least, to keep even pace with the constantly growing knowledge and keep up to date with the latest of every discipline. I just can't do it!"

"Well, that sounded very ambitious, I must say!"

"I really thought I could do it, but it was a bite that was too big to chew."

"I can imagine…. And I have never even thought about the concept of knowledge and that it slowly grows over time, nor that it can be forgotten… very interesting perspective!"

"Well, yeah, I guess. But big parts of my knowledge are obsolete… And if I try to verify it with someone in any area, they all look at me as something extinct. I usually get away with saying that I've read about it in some old book or something."

"What is some knowledge that has been forgotten over time?"

"Most forgotten knowledge gets rediscovered, but not all, at least not yet."

"You are playing with me Roy, name something!"

"One thing that remains forgotten is Atlantis, their way of life, their location."

"Ah, Atlantis, yes, true beauty indeed. And perhaps best it remains forgotten."

"That we agree on. But I have come across some references in poetry and made up stories about the past, but only as a name, and as a glorified place, nothing more."

"Enough to spark curiosity?"

"Of course, but there are no real references to it, and I believe that it is only the name and being glorified that has survived, nothing more."

"Good, then let's hope it is never rediscovered."

"Agreed, Atlantis should stay forgotten and kept that way."

"Imagine how it would affect the world today…"

"Or any future world when technology has developed even beyond my imagination. And my imagination is vivid, I have seen a lot, not excluding the things of or in Atlantis."

"Even worse! Perhaps worth looking into destroying the references that currently exists?"

"I've tried that, but unfortunately it sparked a temporary interest for Atlantis, so I chose to leave it be and hope it will be purged by itself."

Learning everything in reality

Knowledge is a strange thing. It is never fixed. And it does not only change with perspective, it changes with tiny details. And once some details are unfolded, there are still other details that remain in hiding.

And as Roy experienced, if one person would try to accumulate all knowledge, it would take more than a lifetime to acquire it. And as you probably can relate to, knowledge change over time, perhaps your understanding of something has changed during your life, and probably will change more. Keeping up to date with all changes on all areas is an impossible task. Now, if Roy had the ambition to be like an old encyclopaedia, he would probably have mastered it, but that was never his intent, since it was one of the ways he tried to benefit from his immortality and get on top of things to just relax and do as little as possible.

That part of Roy's grand scheme has never fulfilled. He has always had to work and pull his straw to the stack, like everybody else. Even if he from time to time has thought of it as unfair. Everybody else just have to work a lifetime, but he has to work every lifetime. Then again, the others do not gain the benefits of being immortal.

If I ruled the world according to Roy

"I can imagine, it is what you send out into the universe that are manifested. And when you focus your energy on something, that energy reflects up on others."

"Ok, that is beyond me, but I'll take your word for it. There is a lot of things controlling the world it seems."

"It sure is. And what if you controlled it, how would it be and look like?"

"If I ruled the world?"

"Yes."

"A long time ago, I would not have been any different than the common rulers of this world, I'd too have a noble agenda, get caught by the power and end up making sure I gain as much as possible while in power."

"Sounds like most rulers, I'll give you that. But what about now? With your current perspectives on things."

"I don't know, I do not think it could be done. It would mean that I would force my perspectives on people who would help me achieve my goals. That would make me a dictator. And I believe that my perspectives would be so different from the common man, so it would be difficult for everybody to comprehend. Then I would be overthrown, possibly killed."

"You are probably right, but let's say that were not an issue."

"Then I would say that humanity needs a new point of view, that we are heading in the wrong direction. We think only of ourselves and by that, I mean literally, we do not think of ourselves as humans only as individuals. And each decision is taken to serve our own interest. Even if it makes someone else pay a higher price than me, even if it destroys the things around us, for animals, for nature. We are ruthless today. And fortunately, our overall damage has not had a huge impact yet, but I fear it will have in the future. Up to a point where it is too late and irreversible."

"Sounds about right. What can you do to prevent it from going too far?"

"To be honest, not much, one person cannot do any more than his or her own part in the great whole. And all I could hope to do is to reach out and spread an enlightened word to people. Set a seed that can grow on its own and blossom with clarity to each and every individual. Problem now is that everybody believes they are entitled to a lot of things that are wrong. You can buy things at a low price because the person who made it were not paid enough to make a decent living, thus keep trapping that person in a horrible life. But the person who buys the thing does not see that, they only see to their own benefit. I got something, it did not cost me much, so I can spend more on other things. And over time, things have been more common. And the more things we have, the more things we want. And all necessary things are flooded with unnecessary things. And now a days I do not know if people know what things that are necessary and what are not. Everything is treated the same, and not the same in a good way. We waste too many things in vain. Meaning that ages ago, one person used up a certain amount of recourses during a lifetime. Now that amount has more than doubled, and when I look around, there aren't infinite amount of recourses. My biggest fear is that we will not stop this bad circle in time. What will happen the day we use more recourses than the world can provide?"

"You're on to something here, dear Roy."

"I'd better stop talking about it, it only makes me depressed!"

"Or perhaps you should start talking about it?"

"To what end? To be laughed at when trying to convince people of something they do not believe in, like the creator's path society? Claims to know the truth about the creator and the world."

"Do they?"

"Perspective, in a way I guess, but definitely not in a plenty of ways!"

"And they are being laughed at because they are trying to spread their view and their ideas?"

"Yes, and also the entire isolated cult of their ways and the way they practice their believes."

"So, if you ruled the world it would all be different?"

"I'd like to think so! But then again, I do not want to rule the world. I'm not like Phidas, he could fairly and just rule over the dwarves, while keeping his motifs pure and keep on the road he started out on, keeping his persona throughout the duration of his rule."

"But he made mistakes along the way..."

"So, does all of us, even Phidas. But I am not like him. Nor could I ever hope to be."

If Roy ruled the world in reality

Wizard knew that Roy had more in him than Roy thought of himself. But still, the truth is, and perhaps this is not a truth with perspective, that one man or woman, cannot make these types of changes, it is the responsibility of each and every individual. And as long as the common thoughts are on me or us, and not the entire eco-system of the entire planet, or even the universe, then there is not much anybody can do. And to be able to get to that point where an entire society makes a change that affects everybody to a change is typically (and sadly) when more than half of the society is already in ruins.

And just like the Wizard, I might know a thing or two about where this is heading and may or may not have first-hand experience and knowledge. But it is not my place to tell you or anybody else anything about a possible future. Because, let's face it, even the future is a perspective, and any and all choices effect it in various ways. Not only your choices, but the total sum of every choice by every individual alive at this very moment, regardless of race or age. From every living creature for that matter.

This is also why the future is so complex, and effecting the future is really hard. How can any one-person influence everybody at the same time to choose the same thing and work in the same direction? Even if nothing truly is impossible, this at least counts as really, really, really, really hard. Perhaps with a few more reallys in there.

Power and equality according to Roy

"What makes Phidas such a great leader, worthy of the power that comes with it, in your point of view of course?"

"Phidas is one of those who does not want the power but accept the leadership because of duty and obligation. He inherited the power, he never asked for it. And his loyalty towards the dwarf kind makes him want to keep the power away from his brother, and thus, he chooses to reign the dwarf kingdom. Not as king, because he sees his grandfather as the true king, no he chose the title Grand Master. As where his brother immediately took the title King of the northern province. Greedy with power."

"How so?"

"Well, power is of that nature. Greedy. Power attracts more power, and the bigger the power the stronger the urge for more power rises. And the simplicity is that all creatures are created equal. Not the same, not with the same possibilities, but equal. There is no deferens between the life of a bug like a fly or moth, compared to a human or a dwarf. Nor a fish or an eagle. Or flower or tree. All life is created equal, with a purpose in the great whole. Sure, there are natural hierarchies within some species. Like a pack of wolves, led by an alfa male, or a flock of elephants led by an alfa female. In these natural hierarchies the individual animal chooses to give away its own power to the alfa. But it will also get something in return. Bigger chance of food, cover from other hostile animals, shelter, help with rising offspring, bigger chance of finding a mate and so on. And when there is shift in leadership it is the will of the pack, they simultaneously take back their power from the former leader and give it to the new. And the problem with humanity, and the dwarf society, the two societies I know the best, is that we are taught to give away our power to society and taught that there is no possibility to ever take it back. Which there always is. This is the natural order of power. But the power in human society, and dwarf society alike, has grown too big, thus a power failsafe has been established in subjugate the people of the society in to a degree where they truly become slaves to the power in the society. Now the society has lost its original purpose, to serve the people in it, to give them a better life. Now people exist to serve the society and give society more power."

"And this Phidas knows?"

"Well, at least he knows that the dwarves no longer have the choice, and he understands that power in the wrong hands can be devastating to the individuals of the society. His thoughts are to keep the power from those who want it the most and try to give it back to the individuals of the society. But he realised that it is a difficult task. See, once a people of a society has given away their power, lost the notion that the power is theirs to take back whenever they feel like there is a stronger leader they can support, then the people does not want their power back. Once they get it, it feels like they have been given something that does not belong to them and they fight to be relieved of their own power. A part of the power failsafe. Once you have surrendered your power, you have someone to blame, and it is easy to expect somebody else to take responsibility. Everything else becomes someone else's problem. A problem that the society are supposed to fix for you. An enhancement of the natural power, if I give away my power to gain food and the leader does not provide food, then it is a bad leader and I can blame the leader for not taking care of the food issue. And as long as there is no stronger leader that can provide me with food, I keep supporting the existing one. All the while blaming the leader for my lack of food. Food is no longer my concern or responsibility, it is the leader's or the society's responsibility. That's what happens when the leader takes too much power. If the leader only takes as much power as you give, you still have your own responsibilities and obligations. But when the leader takes too much power, you forget about your own responsibilities and obligations and expect the leader to get you everything. And as the leader who gets more power by providing more to your people, the leader naturally keeps providing more and more, to gain more and more power. Then the balance is totally off, and all power is given to the leader. And the leader needs to keep providing everything and anything in order to maintain the power."

"You have given this a great deal of thought, haven't you?"

"Yes, and most of my insights has been given to me here, when I have gained perspective on things."

"Ok, this is very heavy and serious stuff. Tell me a joke!"

Power and equality in reality

*Sleeping people, that's what Vladir always called everybody.
Humans, dwarves and vampires in particular. But also, other
spices. The only ones who weren't sleeping people were those who
needed to sleep the most, the undead. They needed to be put to the
eternal sleep. That was his cause, to try and wake people up from
their powerless slumber. To get everybody to realise that everything
is in their own hands. That was his motivation for the entire Sky
Road project.*

*And rightfully. Most people, all species included, are sleeping. The
power each individual has, both in its own and in the collective is
significant. By giving it away, or rather, not claim it, is a common
fault. And by not recognising the power within, it is easy to
underestimate your own value, and then it is easy for those in
power to trick you into thinking less of yourself and make you
believe in the lie of your lesser value.*

*Over the ages, I have witnessed the development of every possible
species, more than you can imagine. And it is common at first to see
small groups working together, pulling recourses. This usually
works fine until the groups get too large. Then the concept of power
becomes both clear and necessary. And a leader is chosen, either
officially or unofficially. Officially leaders tend to change and be
challenged. Unofficially leaders tend to stay longer, probably
because they most of the time does not want the power. And over
time, power seems to grow, greed feeds power to gain more power.
Then the leaders, chosen or not, gets to carry a heavy burden, while
slowly (most often anyway) becoming poisoned with the burden
power.*

*There once was a wise man who said: 'If you want to make
everybody happy, don't become a leader, sell ice cream.' And I
guess that is one of the downsides of it. Being in power forces you
to make decisions, and there are always those who does not care
about your decision, those who are for it and those who oppose it.
Yes, you guessed correctly, it is because of perspective. We always*

have multiple perspectives in each and every decision, not necessary right or wrong, just different.

A joke according to Roy

"I stayed up all night wondering where the sun went, then it dawned on me!"

A joke according to the Wizard

"Ok, my turn. What is the opposite of firefly?"

"The opposite? I have no clue!"

"Waterfall!"

"Clever! I like it! Do you want to hear Vladir's favourite joke?"

"Hit me!"

A joke according to Vladir

"Why does the trees seem suspicious on sunny days?"

"I don't know!"

"Because they are a bit shady!"

"Good one!"

Almost dying according to Roy

"When we are on the subject of jokes, do you want to hear the story where I almost died?"

"Is death a joke? Or how come you thought of this in this context?"

"Well, it is one of those times where I have laughed the most in my life… hence the joke part, but no, death is not a joke… but let's come back to that, I have studied death and I have some thoughts surrounding that…"

"Ok, but first the story!"

"Alright, it was back in my robbin' days. A few of my associates and me were hiding away some of our hot belongings that needed to cool down for a while before we dared to try and sell it. It was a rainy day, and we have climbed some slippery hills deep in the great forest. We were all soaking wet both from the rain and from the sweat of digging. We were about to cover everything up and the last touch was to try and even out the ground using big blankets of sacks. Me and one of the others were standing and stomping above the blanket when it suddenly slipped away down the hill, sliding in the mud. The both of us fell and was dragged along on the ride. It was like when kids ride something down a hill in the winter, but a lot faster and the two of us caught in the fabric, all tangled in. Our ride was not graceful or short, we caught such speed that we rode all the way to the foot of the hills and further. Only to go full stop against a big rock. On our way down, we passed most of the trees and bushes, but crashed into a few, not slowing down, only a small change in direction. Each encounter leaving us scratched and bruised. Oh, the pain when we hit that rock. We both lay completely still and silent for a while, letting our souls and minds catch up with our bodies, and feeling the pain rush through our bodies as the adrenaline slowly wore off. When we tried to rise, both moaned simultaneously and even if there were nothing laughable in the situation, that's exactly what we did. We laughed our asses off. And if we were in pain and agony before we started to

234

laugh, it was nothing in comparison. The more we laughed the more it hurt, and the more it hurt, the more we laughed."

"A common stress reaction, laughing uncontrollably when the situation is resolved."

"Whatever it was I have never laughed so much in my entire life… even after I healed, which were significantly faster than my friend, I was still sour every time I laughed. And back then, I used to laugh a lot… there are so much misery among thieves back then that the smallest scours of laughter were brought right in the centre of attention."

"You laughed death in its face!"

"Almost literally, I cannot explain how we survived that ride, but we did, and I feel it was like cheating death a little. But since my friend also survived, I know for sure that it was not my immortality that saved me."

"Perhaps it saved the both of you?"

"How do you mean?"

"There is a lot of the life essence and the effects of it that you do not know yet…"

"And this is not the time to get enlightened?"

"No, but there will be…"

Almost dying in reality

Yes, there would come a time for enlightenment, or rather, many occasions. And in this particular moment, the enlightenment would stand for the reason that Roy and his friend did not die that day. There are many creatures of the multiverse, and now I do not speak of creatures that inhabit different worlds, because they obviously exist. You are one, I would be one, or maybe was one. I am talking about creatures of the multiverse that exist on a different spectrum than we do. That are there, but then again, not really there. Not visible to the naked eye, not occupying space like we do, but none the less a living creature. Like the Wizard. One of many different types of creatures and all with different purpose, different talents, personalities, different, well, everything.

In this case the reason for not dying was Angels, and a particular kind of angel, namely guardian angels. Angels are a mixture of creatures supporting life in the multiverse. They are all drawn to life essence. Guardian Angels have a specific task. They protect life essence by altering the energy surrounding events in the multiverse. And as they alter energy, things happen in a different way. Their interference is always in the interest of serving the life essence. Keeping it, not letting it go to waste. The more life essence in one place, the more guardian angels. The truth of that magic carpet-ride that day would have been a certain death to both Roy and his friend. But the amount of guardian angels that surrounded them both, helped them out, fulfilling their purpose in the multiverse, and it still was close that they did not make it.

The expression 'touched by angel hands' refer to experiences like this one, only when you are touched by angel hands, you get a super tiny amount of their energy transferred to your being. The effect wears off after a while, but during the moment it lasts, people often feel very happy, lightened of all burdens, filled with an inner calm. In this case, they had so much of the angel's energy that their bodies and souls only way to channel it was through laughter. Laughter is one of the most powerful expressions the soul and body can join forces in producing. Other strong forces like love is only an expression of the soul, while lust is the expression of the body.

Oh no, now I am rambling about everything again, sorry. I should stick to the story.

Death according to Roy

"Ok, Mr Secret-Know-it-all, now I would like to talk about death a little while."

"I am looking forward to hear it."

"And before I start, I assume that there are things you know that you will not share with me."

"As always!"

"Glad we got that out of the way, and if you, at any time, feel like filling me in on something, explain something or answer any question I might have, I promise I will not hold it against you and certainly not give you a hard time for enlightening me."

"Noted."

"As you can imagine, I have seen quite a few deaths throughout my life."

"A quick pass, ironic expression, 'seen quite a few' when you really mean many… continue…"

"Ok, but don't interrupt me with that kind of stuff, only when you can add something of value… and as I said, I have seen many deaths in my life. And after a while I have started to see certain patterns. Death is not just death, it can come expected of old age or illness, and those deaths have some things in common, it can come unexpected by illness, accidents or deliberate actions from others. And those have some things in common."

"The people that are inflicting their deliberate actions or the unexpected deaths?"

"The ladder, and don't interrupt me I said."

"Ok, I'll try to keep quiet."

"Try? Isn't it a choice?"

"Now you're only mocking me!"

"Indeed, I am! And I enjoy it too!"

"I can tell, but go on… I'll *choose* to be quiet unless I can enlighten you…"

"As I were saying, different kinds of deaths, expected and unexpected. Those who expect it usually leave this life with a calm expression once they have died. Those who are unexpected leave a troubled expression once they have died. Any idea why that might be?"

"Yes, but I'll cannot share that information right now."

"Ok, but I have a thought on that. I get a feeling that when we die, expected or unexpected alike, there is something that leaves the body. I have been thinking that it might be the life essence."

"Why do you figure that?"

"Well, for one thing, the black witches extracted it from living people. Causing a great deal of pain and harm. It would be easier for them to extract it from dead people. But they didn't, so I figure that the life essence is no longer present in us when we die."

"Solid conclusion. I will not confirm it, but the reasoning behind it sounds sound."

"Furthermore, I believe, and this is a pure speculation, but I cannot help but feeling it might be right. The soul. I do not believe it dies. I believe that it simply moves on to some other place or something. And based on what you've told me about the multiverse today, it strengthens my beliefs."

"Also, sound reasoning. But I will not confirm it, should it be true."

"That being said. It could be a possibility to meet my wife and child again… but only if that place is where the souls of dead people spend eternity. And I do not think that would be the case, since that place would be very crowded as time passes."

"And here I need to point out that time both passes and does not. It is your perception that the time passes, and it is not untrue, but it is not true either."

"Ok, that did not help. But I can confess that when I started to think that there was a tiny possibility to see my family again, I was completely ready to end my own life, just to be with them again."

"But you didn't… obviously, why?"

"Well, even if I believe this very strongly, I do not have any proof or anything that confirms my thoughts other than this tiny feeling inside saying I am right. And I cannot verify it in any other way then to end my life. And what if I am wrong? Then I have only wasted my own life."

"I'm glad you haven't wasted your own life, it has mattered throughout time, and it will still matter for ages to come…"

"You say I have a purpose to fill?"

"No, rather multiple purposes, but that is not because you are immortal, that is just the nature of every life…"

"Ok, I'm special, but not *that* special?"

"Oh, but don't get me wrong, you certainly are that special. The multiverse would not have been the same without you, or will be the same, from your perspective."

Death in reality

Death is another creature of the multiverse… but unlike the angels that are drawn to life essence in order to protect it, death is draw to life essence to return it to the multiversal scours. And it also has another mission, guiding the souls to their next assignment. Something I do not know anything about. Now, I want to stress out, many people blame death for taking away their loved ones. But it is not true, death has no right nor mandate to decide who dies or who lives, death is only carrying out his tasks, to be present at the point of death to collect life essence and to guide a soul who just lost its temporary home in a body of some sort.

Now, death is a very sensitive creature, and is strict to its duties, but every now and then, when it's not the multiversal beings that decides who will live and who will die, when creatures take the matter of life and death into their own hands, then it can be very busy times for death. Like in a war, or when two clans have a disagreement, then death have very busy times. And as a multiversal creature, death is not bound by time, but it still happens that a soul gets lost along the way because death is not there to guide it. That is failure that death takes very seriously, and it hunts the lost soul down in order to guide it back on the right track. But once in a while, the lost souls stay lost despite death's best attempts to guide it right.

And as for Roy, he thought more than once to end his own life to be reunited with his family. But luckily, he never followed through with that thought.

Immortal and above the law according to Roy

"Riddle-man. What I don't understand is that Everything you see, past, present, future, not only that, but all the possible outcomes of it all, simultaneously... All that is hard to take in and logically I could possibly understand it, but I don't believe that I ever will take it all in..."

"Is there a question in there?"

"Yes, what I am trying to get to is that even if we all have choices, and each choice leads to a different outcome, and that there theoretically would mean that there are an infinite amount of Roy's sitting on a mountainside at this moment, and an even greater number of Roy's that are doing other things, there does not seem to be any loopholes..."

"I don't understand, what do you mean?"

"Well, I could argue that everything is predestined, no matter what I choose, there is always a road ahead that is already mapped out, except I do not know it. And no matter what I do, the only thing I can do is change the road I will follow, I can never do anything to break that road structure. I am predestined to walk those different roads, I can never create a new road and choose to walk that road."

"Well, as usual you are both right and wrong. As of now, you are completely right. But keep in mind that you are evolving, slowly, but already at this point, you are significantly different from other humans."

"Maybe that is why I do not feel like I belong or need to obey the laws of man?"

"Please elaborate."

"Well, I don't feel like I need to obey the laws of men. Whatever law or rule, written or unwritten, it doesn't apply to me, I can break

242

it without any real repercussions. If I am put into jail, I will outlive everybody that put me there and if I am banned from a place, I can visit it again as time has passed. Whatever punishment is thrown at me, except maybe decapitation or something like that, I will conquer it."

"Ah, immortal and lawless."

"In a way… and that is a feeling that is growing on me, but still I am limited by my choices and predestined only to choose from the possible roads ahead of me."

"Perhaps. And if nothing else, that is the way your current situation is, but like I said, and it might be saying too much, you are evolving, and as evolution keeps working on you, you will undoubtedly change. Into who or what is uncertain, but I can say as much. There is a point in time where I lose track of you. Where you vanish of the radar of the entire multiverse. I do understand why, but I do not understand how. It is as if you break the structure of the multiverse itself. And the odd thing is, that chronologically speaking, you still exist after that point in time. Only not as before."

"So, you are saying that it is possible that I can create my own road and chose to walk that instead."

"Perhaps, it is a reasonable parable. But as usual, it is far more complex than that."

"I cannot possible comprehend it now, but I believe this information will inspire me in the future, at least that is what it feels like now."

"You may very well be right. And as we have had this dialogue, the future has shifted significantly."

"So, you are also creating new roads, merely by speaking to me?"

"You could say so. Speaking to you is affecting the fundamental structure of the multiverse, but that is the nature of my being. Thus, it could be a result of my actions rather than your actions, or future actions… it is hard to tell, and not even I can make heads or tale of what comes first, the hen or the egg. Not figuratively speaking, because I know the hen was created first, and then the hen laid an egg. But you know what I mean."

Immortal and above the law in reality

Roy's feeling that he did not belong with the rest of the people of this world was a natural development, and a key to coming events. Being immortal does something to the way you think, it changes the foundation of your perspectives to something that is unimaginable to a mortal being. The prospect of being alive forever can only overload your thoughts. Then, as you live through it, experience immortality over time, your thoughts catch up, slowly, and gradually you change.

This experience took time for Roy, not because he was more stupid than anybody else, nor slower than others, but his mind actively resisted it and tried to deny it, reject it from the very beginning. And it is only logically that the things you embrace affects you stronger and quicker than things you oppose. At least when it comes to your own choices and thoughts. Roy was clinging on to the last straws of mortality for way longer than most people would have. Which is probably also the reason it did not raise to his head and made him arrogant and thinking he was better than everybody else.

By letting his mortality stay with him for as long as he could made him rather humble to eternity and respecting the nature of his new state in a different way.

As for standing above the law, no member of society can ever stand above the law. If that would be the case, then the foundation of a society would fall, bringing the entire society with it. Even so, the feeling was real and true to Roy, his perspective would change over time. Immortal or not, if an individual chose to be part of a society, the person needs to respect the law of that very society. Which is not the same as saying Roy was wrong in his thoughts, they were still true, but as time passed and wisdom came, Roy used the very same thoughts to motivate himself to respect the laws rather than to see himself above it. Right or wrong, always a perspective.

The mother tree according to Roy

"Speaking of which… I have encountered a special tree on this world. It has a special connection to this world. Does it provide the world with its energy or does the world provide it with its energy?"

"Ah, you mean the mother tree?"

"The mother tree?"

"Yes, every planet has one. All different, but essential to each planet."

"Would the world die if it were damaged or cut down?"

"Look at it like this. A world, like a person, is combined with many components, where the planet would be equivalent to a worlds body. And if you take a person you have life essence and soul, only to mention a few of all the things that make up a person. Same goes for a planet. Inside each planet is a core, normally containing the planets life essence, only it is not life essence, it is most often concentrated energy and matter in various frequencies. Some harmonizing, some not so much. The mother tree has both roots to stay strong and steady, to drink water from the ground *and* a completely different kind of roots that goes all the way down to the core. But it is not physical roots that you can cut off like the roots drinking water. The purpose of these second types of roots is to channelize energy from the planets core throughout all parts of the planet."

"So, what you are saying is that if it is hurt, the energy of the planet stops being channelized and the planet dies?"

"No, on the contrary. The tree itself is indeed significant to the energy flow of every planet, but it is 'just' the top of a wide and deep network of roots."

"Then what happens if something happens to the tree?"

"What do you think?"

"Well, I don't know what I think, but I can tell you what I've seen."

"Well, what have you seen then?"

"I've seen the mother tree cut down and destroyed."

"What happened?"

"Nothing. At least not right away. At first, for the next few days the ground got darker and lost almost every growing thing, then after a week or so, two new trees started to grow where the first tree had been standing. And it just took a few days to the two new trees to grow tall, as if they had been there for ages."

"Now, what does this tell you?"

"I guess it tells me that if you cut down a mother tree, two more trees take its place."

"And why would that be?"

"Maybe because the planets energy still needs to balance itself through the roots of the mother tree?"

"Good, just about right. For each tree that is cut down, two more grows up, and in theory the entire surface of a planet could be covered in mother trees."

"Would it be good or bad?"

"Neither good nor bad. It would just be what it is."

"But if mother trees cover all the surface of a planet, then nothing else would be able to grow?"

"Precisely."

"Isn't that bad?"

"From what perspective?"

"From the perspective of all the other species that used to live there?"

"In that case bad."

"How could it be good?"

"If you look at it from the perspective of the planet and the mother trees."

"I guess. But what about the energy? Would it drain the core quicker with all the surface covered in channels from the core?"

"It would!"

"Then what?"

"The planet would die."

"But then it would be bad."

"From what perspective?"

"From the planet's perspective."

"Well, yes, but think about what could emerge in the space currently occupied by a planet…"

"What would that be?"

"Can't tell you, you wouldn't understand."

"I'd love another opportunity to say I don't understand!"

The mother tree in reality

Truth be told, Roy did not just watch the first mother tree get cut down and be destroyed, he cut it down and used it as logs to a night fire.
In his defence it was dark, and he thought the small glowing was light from the moons. And it was not until it started burning that he understood it was something different with this particular tree. And the heat from that tree was something he never felt again in his entire life, not even from the breath of a dragon.

He thought to himself that this wood would be perfect for the mines of the dwarves. Too bad there were only one.

And when he visited the same place a few days later, he was astounded that there were two new trees in the place where he cut down the first.

Then he knew it was something special with that tree, or those two trees. And ages later when he visited the place for the third time, there were three trees where he found the first, long time ago.

Now, exactly what happens when you cut down a mother tree, I do not know, but I do know this, the life will of those trees and the entire underground network of energy roots is very powerful and will find new ways to prosper. Mother tree or not.

The never-ending road according to Roy

"I bet you do, but not this one. To horrid and too complicated for the time being."

"Ok, I give up, what's our next topic?"

"I don't know. But I feel kind of bad, keeping you out in the dark on so many things."

"If you say so I will take advantage of this situation."

"In what way?"

"I'll ask you something that puzzles me, that I am assuming that is not too big of a secret, and you'll tell me…"

"Perhaps, nothing I can promise in advance, what do you have in mind?"

"The never-ending road…"

"The never-ending road?"

"There is a spot on a road, far from where you hid the house, where you just cannot go forward, no matter how many steps you take or how much time you spend on going forward."

"Oh, tell me more…"

"The spot is widely known, but no one can explain it, not even the mightiest wizards of this world. Now a days it marked and there is a path leading around the area. No matter what direction you take, it is the same. And an odd thing is that even if the entire world is covered by winter, this spot will always have a sunny summer day. And if it is raining outside, the sun is shining in this spot."

"Ah… I know what this is. And I can gladly tell you about it."

"That is some piece of good news! What about it?"

"Well, I'll try to explain it as simple as possible. You know time and how it can be compared to a steady floating river?"
"Yes..."

"Imagine that somewhere along the bottom, typically near the riverbank, there is an oddly shaped rock, not just any rock, but one that is shaped in a certain way. That rock makes the stream of the water turn and go backwards, creating a swirl in the river."

"Yes, I've seen those, almost every running water has them, tiny streams or big rivers. Even oceans."

"Oceans? No, I believe those swirls are of a different kind, but that is beside the point. Now, think of the time, running into a big timewave that has great impact on the timeline, like the one that took you back in time. Even if time is not matter, it is energy. And as those two fronts of energy collides, they create a new energy that are moving in a different direction than everything in the surroundings. When this happens to time, it is called a time bubble. Since matter is not the same as time, matter can move in and out of this bubble. But time itself cannot. So, inside this bubble it is the same timeframe all the time, could be minutes, could be hours, even days. The point is that time is still moving. Had it not been, it had affected matter as well, and any matter that would have entered the bubble would not be able to move."

The never-ending road in reality

A truly strange place, the never-ending road. It was discovered by accident. Shortly after building the road some of the workers were heading back to pick up some tools they'd left along the way. Two of them were walking a bit further, and three of them came behind with a horse driven wagon to load everything on.

The ones with the wagon stopped at a distance behind the two scouts and laughed at them, because they seemed to goof around and kept walking on the same spot. But after a while it was rather clear that they weren't goofing and one of the others walked in and joined his companions in the never-ending walk. Only problem was that as each person walks into the bubble, the same person is in the claws of the bubble, without the possibility escape. And even if the three-man strong party tried to walk their way back, they did not move in either direction. Stuck in the time vortex and would still be if the two remaining men hadn't acted as they did. They sent one man in with a rope tied around his waist, the other end was tied in the wagon and using the wagon, the fifth man could pull all the other four out of the time vortex. They built a fence around it and put up warning signs. Even so, a few have been stranded in the vortex without the possibility to escape by themselves. Now a days there are fixed rescue ropes that can be used to pull people out. But it is common knowledge not to enter beyond the warning fence.

The day that time stopped according to Roy

"Then I need to interrupt with a question, or perhaps a story related to that question."

"Oh, let's hear it!"

"I have had an experience once, then never again. And it was really odd. I was the only one to experience it."

"What was it."

"It was as if time itself stood still, everybody around me just froze. People, animals, even the leaf's blowing in the wind, and the wind itself. Everything completely still. I could not breath, but I could move. And I have always figured that it had something to do with the time stopping, but if it stopped, you just said that it affected matter as well, and nothing would be able to move."

"Hmm… interesting… how was the experience?"

"It was quite terrifying. I was the only one who could move around, while everybody in the whole town, outside as well as inside just stopped in whatever they were doing. Even the fires in the fireplaces and on the town-square just stopped, or rather, froze, there was still heat coming from it, but the flames did not move."

"And you didn't see anything, or anyone move during this time?"

"No, not a single thing or any person."

"How did it end?"

"Well, I was scared as never before, almost had a panic attack, and I walked around planless just looking at everything, walking from building to building, room to room just… I don't know, was not really thinking clear, anyway, as sudden as it had started it stopped. And as it did, I was in front of a woman in her own home as she was dressing from her bath. From her point of view, I must have appeared out of thin air. Naturally she screamed, and her husband that were in the living area came to her rescue. I was taken for a burglar or a rapist and was treated accordingly. Took me a few days to recover from that beating."

"I can only think of one powerful enough to pull something like that off, but I see no motifs for her to do it…"

"Leola?"

"Oh, no, not by far… and besides, there is no telling if it was a created event, or a natural cause. There are natural phenomena that would appear like this. And nobody notices it, since everything is affected. But the odd thing here is that you weren't affected. That in itself speaks for a created event. Then again, you have previous experiences with timewaves, which could explain why you were not affected by it. Hard to tell. I am sorry, I cannot give you a conclusive answer on this."

"Yet another mystery then?"

"Well, I have to think about it for a while. And remember."

"My theory has been that time also can freeze, like water turning to ice. Only this happened instantly on both transactions, not slowly as when water freezes."

"Hmm… interesting theory. Should it be true I can think of more possibilities as to why it happened."

"Natural cause, somebody, not Leola was behind it or several more possibilities?"

"Yes, that's right!"

"You know, you aren't exactly helping out here…"

"I'm sorry, it's just that I do not know…"

"Thought you knew everything?"

"Oh no, not by far. I am merely a Wizard of the multiverse, and there are plenty of things I do not know or are able to do… there is no such thing as an all knowing being who can do everything. It is the combination and balance of everything that keeps things in order. Not a single being."

The day that time stopped in reality

The matter of the fact was that it was created, not natural occurring, and it was one of the most powerful wizards of this world that was behind it. Yes, you've heard her name before, and you will hear it again. Ora.

She did not mean anything by it, but she thought she had seen it happen naturally and tried to recreate it, successfully I might add. She was in the village as she performed her magic. She did not see Roy move, if so, she would have been very surprised. And since she had no hidden agenda, just curiosity, she just tried it to see if she could. And as she had successfully shown it to herself and proved her theory, she let it go, and never performed it again. Even if she could do it, she saw no reason to do it again, besides, she was uncertain how it would affect time over all if she kept freezing it, so she'd rather not do it again, due to her lack of knowledge and seeing the full picture.

Had she tried it more, she would see that her stunts would have very little impact on the overall time and events, only minor changes would occur.

...and Roy was genially surprised to hear that even the Wizard had limitations. He'd started to believe that the Wizard was the all-knowing force in the multiverse, but oh, how wrong he was. And it was a good lesson to learn at that point. It would come in handy later.

Swirls in the ocean according to Roy

"What about the swirls of the ocean, is that something I can learn today?"

"Yes, my friend, at last something I can explain! Feels good to be back on track again!"

"I must say, I am surprised, I thought you could explain everything, do anything and knew just about everything there is to know."

"No, far from it, my friend! I know a lot, can influence a lot, but even I have my limits!"

"It's good to know, you tell me stuff, you are clear when you know but do not want to tell me, and also when you do not know. I feel confident in our dialogues, I know where you stand in everything and can both accept and respect your point of view in everything!"

"Well, thank you! It warms my heart to hear you say so!"

"No, how about those ocean swirls?"

"Yes, those… natural phenomena. Created by variations in underwater currents, both speed and direction. By temperature. By wind direction and windspeed, and last, but certainly not least, the sun with its heating beams."

"Huh, I was hoping for a big hole in the ocean floor."

"Yeah, that would be something, but where would all the water go?"

"I don't know, through the underground and released as mist or snow on a mountaintop?"

"Interesting thought, and plausible…"

"Especially if you add the dwarf knowledge that the further down you come, the hotter it gets, then it's not far-fetched that the water would boil, and boiling water becomes mist. And there are several mountaintops with mist. And as mist cools down it transforms to ice or snow, and both are known to exist on mountaintops, even in summer."

"It is quite the logic! You've really given this a lot of thought, haven't you?"

"Yeah, some... I mean, as you said, plausible..."

"I will try that on some world, to see if it is possible. Do you want me to get back to you with that?"

"I'd love that! I mean, everything around us is based on cycles, so why not that?"

"You surprise me, dear Roy. I did not see that coming from you!"

"Well, you know what they say, even a blind chicken occasionally finds a seed while picking the ground..."

"What is that I hear from you? Where did this modesty come from all of a sudden?"

"I don't know. Just nothing I ever imagined talking to anybody about..."

"You know what? This is why I enjoy having these talks with you... you give me so much that I've never thought of before, not to say all the different perspectives you provide..."

Swirls in the ocean in reality

Roy really had given this a lot of thought, and it was a tough blow to take, getting his theory dismissed like that. But also, a great confirmation that his idea might actually work and would be tested out.

And Roy later got a message from the Wizard, a message that was undoubtedly a confirmation that his theory worked, but no one around him understood what it was all about. Only Roy. But that is a story for another time. Nothing we'll talk about here.

Living versus surviving according to Roy

"I'm flattered."

"Ah, you should be, I enjoy our talks…"

"You say talks… but from my perspective this is our first. Not our first encounter, but our first talk."

"Well, what can I say? There will be more to come, from your perspective. After all, you have lived a long life, and if all goes well, you'll have a long life a head."

"Can you tell me something about it?"

"Of course not, but you can tell me this. Now you've been sitting on this rock for far longer than humanly possible and immortally healthy… how does it feel?"

"Well, I can only say that when I live as I am supposed to, it feels good and everything is fine. That is live itself… but now, I force my body to do the extreme, yes, I survive, but I do not live… and that is a huge difference, I can tell you!"

"I can imagine, but tell me…"

"Well, every part of my body and every system is stretched to the max. My body's only life supporting system, besides oxygen at the moment, is the extra amount of life essence that I carry inside. Rest of my resources are all gone. All my systems should have failed by now, but the life essence keeps everything running, even if it is just on a tiny fraction of each systems normal capacity. Nothing ever stops running completely."

"Rather amazing, and really all we talk about is an imbalance that have a tremendous impact on you…"

"Yeah, but it feels awful not to live, to only survive, nothing I would recommend to anyone."

"But still amazing. I mean, now, in a while, you will just rise and walk over to the others and re-join where you left off. And I am willing to bet that they will not notice much on you, that your entire body will be fully awake and fully functional by only taking that short walk…"

"And I have planned this well, each step, I will start to go downward a bit, to a tiny stream. Wash myself, cut my hair and beard, drink like I were about to moist an entire desert, and then, if all goes well, change clothing. I've left a pile of new clothing in a hidden sack under a rock. If it is still there and the cloth has not been ruined by nature, I will have fresh clothes to were as I re-join the others."

"But of course, it feels completely natural when you say you've planned this to the detail, but somehow I just imagined that you would get up and walk straight to meet the others."

"Well, that is what I would have had to do unless, at last moment, I came to think of how to make a first impression when I am not expected to do one. From their point of view, I have not been away, and imagine the looks of their faces if I would come back looking as a beggar or something. Then they would really start wondering what had happened. Figure I'd better get back there about the same as I left."

"Good thinking! Do you remember what clothes you had when you disappeared?"

"No, not the slightest, so I gambled on something that I used to wear a lot, white shirt in linen and brown pants with a black leather belt."

"Sounds about right. But I think you had a vest as well…"

"Bummer, I did not think about that…"

"Well, if it is any comfort, it is not a big deal if someone takes off their vest in temperatures like this… I'm sure no one will notice…"

"Let's hope so!"

Living versus surviving in reality

Oh yes, there is a big difference between surviving and living. And what Roy did not mention is that living is not only about the physical parts with eating, moving, breathing, it is also the interaction with others, all the feelings that run through mind and body.

And at the time of this conversation, Roy had been lonely for so long that he had gotten used to his own company and his own thoughts, and it was not until he freshened up by the stream and got into his "new" clothes that he realised that there was much more to say about living versus surviving, but then it was too late, the conversation was already had, and that is another lesson in life. It is what you do or say in the moment that forms the reality, it is not what you could have our should have said and done. It is always what you do *in the moment.*

My apologies, now I am rambling on about other things again. It is not my intention, only my thoughts wandering about. Sometimes I forget that it is not me... ah, never mind... let's just carry on with the story, shall we?

The power of talking according to the Wizard

"Have you thought about what to say at first?"

"Hi, I suppose. And I'm not sure what I'm walking into… I am uncertain of how Groll's death will have impacted everyone. I mean, different for each one, of course, but, well I don't know…"

"No, carry on… I think you are on to something…"

"I don't know, I just… it feels as if this would be one of those moments where the conversation has a really big impact. This is no time for saying or doing something wrong, everything has to be just right, and balanced."

"Maybe…"

"What do you mean?"

"Well, a conversation is not always about talking you know…"

"What do you mean?"

"You can be a part of the conversation with your ears as well…."

"What do you mean?"

"I mean listening…"

"Listening?"

"Yes, listening is the utter most important thing in a meaningful conversation. And listening to understand not to reply…"

"Huh… but doesn't the conversation get really one-sided if one part is only in it to listen?"

"No, listening means a chance to really understand, and understanding get the conversation to a whole other level. Genuinely care for another person, or another being. Conversation is not only what you say…"

"Interesting, I need to try that, sounds like something that will be useful."

"Well, at least it is something that cuts all the bull shit and focus on what really matters."

"And what would that be?"

"The truth behind the mask, the real person, the feelings and the reactions. Sharing those. It is called empathy. And when you have that as your focus in your conversation the focus shifts from what this person can do for me to what can I learn from this person… it shifts the entire balance of both power and reason for the conversation."

"Assuming it is honestly meant, and that there is no hidden agenda in listening…"

"Assuming both parties are open and honest… Vulnerable…"

"Well, if you let down your mask, or guard, and reveal your true self, you are vulnerable. This means that the other person can do real damage to you if they want to, you have opened up to that. You have left you comfort zone and stepped outside it. Leaving you vulnerable."

"Sounds hard to do… I mean, who would be brave enough to take the first step into something like that, without knowing if the other person will hurt you… that is some serious trust."

"But who will ever take the first step of nobody dares to do it."

"Nobody!"

"Exactly, and how do you think a conversation can get to this point if no one dares to start?"

"It is simply impossible."

"Yes, so if you want to gain this incredible way of meeting another person, you need to dare to be vulnerable and truthful. This also means you cannot be perfect and have everything figured out. Because there is no such person. Nobody is perfect."

"So, there is an egoistic agenda behind it?"

"No, not at all, just a desire to truly meet another person without everything that normally stands in the way."

"It sounds great, but I'm still sceptical."

"You need to try and practice to get good at it, and when you are good at it, this will not only enrich your life, but also enrich the lives of the people you talk to."

The power of talking in reality

This very conversation was a defining moment in Roy's life. Not that he identified that at first, but over time, this insight changed Roy's thoughts about life and relations fundamentally. And it took years and years of practice before he could say that he had reached a basic knowledge of the power of talking, and lifetimes to perfect it. Luckily for Roy, he had lifetimes to spend on it. But in this book series, Roy will not have come so far in his development yet, so you probably will not notice anything more than perhaps tiny details in behavioural change.

But in the fourth book of this series, where you'll meet up with Roy and the others again, and occasionally Roy reminds himself of this conversation and tries to use the knowledge in it, to get closer to the person he is talking to, perhaps for the wrong reasons, but his desire is pure.

Again, I am getting ahead of myself, so try not to pay much attention to me, skip directly to the next passage of this book so you don't have to spend any more time or energy on my rambling.

Still here are you, well, I guess that I perhaps has sparked an interest for something that you will not find the answer to here, as promised, they will be found later on, as the overall story keeps building up and eventually continues.

Roy talking the talk according to the Wizard

"It's strange, I've always thought I was good at talking."

"Don't get me wrong, you are! This is just a different way of looking at it."

"A different perspective?"

"Yes, and you have a true gift in talking!"

"Yeah, I guess, I've never had problems with filling space with words. And I've had good experiences talking my way out of any situation... Well, most of the times anyway."

"This far you've been a quantity man... Good with words, always picking the right ones, depending on who you are talking to. And like you said, never a problem filling spaces with words. Eliminating silences."

"When you say it like that, it does not sound like a good thing."

"With the silences?"

"Nor with a running mouth."

"Perspective remember... that is the important thing, you can twist and turn on anything to get it both good and bad. And it is not even that, just different perspectives..."

"What's the good parts of my talking then?"

"Those you have already described, like talking your way out of almost any situation..."

"Yeah, I guess..."

"And as I said, you adapt to the person you talk to in a marvellous way!"

"I guess, but none of that feels any good now that I know there are a better way…"

"There's the perspective again, not a better way, a different way."

"Yeah, but both myself and others would gain from that way, you said it yourself!"

"True, and now we're back to choice. You can choose to embrace what I said and try to make a change for the better, challenge yourself, develop yourself. Or you can choose to see the negative side of what I said, and, as you do now, let it bring you down instead of using it to build you up."

"Perspective, choice…"

"Yes, and do not mix in right or wrong in this. Everything is what it is, and there is nothing good or bad with that, nothing right or wrong. It's just what it is."

"Are you saying this to cheer me up?"

"No, not really, that is also for you to choose. I may or may not have my reasons for saying things to you, as does everybody else. What you do with what is said to you is totally up to you!"

"Huh, I've never thought about it like that before."

Roy talking the talk in reality

This was the first time throughout the conversation that Roy did not feel good when talking to the Wizard. Later, he would grasp this to be one of those real conversations that actually had an impact on him and embraced the feeling. He said it to be both enjoyable and hard at the same time; enjard. It later became one of his favourite feelings, enjard. Ever so challenging and far out of the comfort zone.

An amazing gift, both receiving and giving. A conversation that really matters, that confirms you as a person, that is true and gives you context and meaning, belonging, seeing others and letting others see you. Amazing on so many levels.

Not that Roy had any problems talking before, he had the gift of talking his whole life, and it was this conversation with the Wizard that eventually lead to develop his gift to something even greater. And that is also something to remember, giving and receiving through conversation is a delicate thing. Conversation can easily turn into something that puts one or both parties in deafens position, which is not good for the conversation. Broaden the perspectives and let go of prestige and your conversations can rise to a whole new level. Let your conversations enjard you!

Ha! I sound like a salesman trying to get you to buy this product, and I am pushing really hard to get you to see how amazing it is. The only trouble for me in this sales pitch is that you are the one who needs to put in all the hard work and take a step out your comfort zone. And what kind of product sells itself when asked to do a bunch of uncomfortable stuff and change a bunch of things? Perhaps more like a religious belief than a product.

Oh, that's me rambling on... Sorry! Again!

The meaning of life according to Roy

"No offence, but there are a lot of things you haven't thought about…"

"I am sure there are plenty of things, but one thing I have thought about a great deal…"

"What is that?"

"The meaning of life!"

"Ah, a classic big question."

"Yeah, I guess everybody touches it periodically during their life, naturally, I have touched by it plenty of times."

"I'm sure you have, and out of curiosity, have you been able to answer it?"

"I have developed several theories over the ages, but I have not been able to verify any of the possible answers. Perhaps you can?"

"Oh, no, life is too great a mystery."

"Is that something you say because you know the answer but won't share it, or do you really not know?"

"Who knows?"

"Well, not me anyway, because you won't tell me… anyway… I have three different approaches to the answer."

"Let's hear them."

"The first approach is a reflection of my first lifetime, before you dragged me back in time. And it is to live life to its fullest and enjoy it as much as possible. The consequence of this life is that it is an egoistic way of life, and result in many questionable choices that have negative impact on other, while having mostly positive impact on my life. The purpose being enjoying life."

"And the second?"

"After hearing many believers talking about the creator's way and taking the high road, always choosing what is right, to one self, to others and to the creation, and that the sum of every action will either affect me positively or negatively. Downside of this is that it may limit yourself, preventing you from your full potential because you show consideration to everything and everyone. The purpose being living a good life and make the right choices.

"Hmm… interesting, and this even if you know that the believes of this world is based on wrong facts about the creator and you know the truth behind these myths?"

"Yes, because however I twist and turn it, even if it is not true as fact, I can still see the truth from the perspective of life. It brings a positive feeling to the believer and it does not cause any harm. Well, for most people, there are of course those who take their believes far too long and go extreme. Then it is not a positive thing anymore. From my point of view."

'Now I'm curious about the third."

"This is based on a mix of the other two, where it loosens up the strictness of the high road on the high horse but keeping the good perspective. And at the same time enjoy life and do what is best for you. But there is a conflict in me saying that the good of it all is lessened as the 'truth' behind it still must be true, and not taking the high road defies the 'truth'.

"Difficult balance… and may I offer a fourth perspective that might be a fourth perspective, or replace or blend with one of the others?"

"Please do, but tell me, is it the truth you are sharing?"

"I cannot say, but the fourth perspective being that life itself is the greatest force in the multiverse, moving forward like a river, with its purpose being only to thrive and continue flowing, and that everything is products of the life's movements. People, plants, animals, worlds, dimensions, everything 'just' a consequence of life itself."

"Wow, that is an exciting perspective."

"And here is yet another; what if the meaning of life is to get to know yourself and communicate with others in the best possible way?"

"Could also be a meaning that would make great deal of sense, because if everybody knew their self, was honest about it and communicated it to other, and at the same time listened to others, it would be a whole lot of difference in this world."

"And imagine if that would be true throughout the multiverse?"

"I only got one word for you: Harmony!"

The meaning of life in reality

The truth about the Wizard and his knowledge was that he does not know. Even if he is a mighty being of the multiverse, the mystery of life itself is beyond him. And even if he talks about being vulnerable and having meaningful conversation, it does not suit him, according to himself, to show sides of him that does not portray him as all powerful.

And another truth is that no one does have a 'true' answer, but many have an answer that is 'true' to themselves. And even if the difference of answers does not point in the same direction, the one 'true' answer does not make the other 'true' answer false, despite their contradictions.
Life is the great mystery of the multiverse even to Roy as immortal and to the Wizard as a being of the multiverse, and perhaps the most important thing is to find your own truth and not trying to live by others truths, after all, you are the one who will have to live with all your choices and it is not up to you to judge anybody else for their choices, and not for them to judge yours.

Music according to Roy

"That's right!"

"And that makes me think about music and instruments, and how we talked about everything being frequencies or vibrations…"

"Oh, this will be interesting, I'm all ears!"

"No, you're not! I am not sure what you are, but you are not all ears! You have a face with a nose and eyes and a long beard and bushy eyebrows, thin hair on your head…"

"Touché, good Roy! Did not see that one coming, and I bow to you! Namaste! I'd very much like to listen to what you have to say!"

Both laughed for a while.

"And you shall. I was thinking. And please help me fill in the blanks or correct my facts. An instrument, it creates sound through vibrations, either vibrations on a string on a violin or a guitar, or by air, like in a flute."

"Yes, right so far."

"And when instruments play together, the sounds, or notes, either fit together and create a harmony, or they do not work well together and sound awful."

"Partly right, but yes… continue…"

"What's only partial right?"

"The part where it sounds awful, that's perspective and preference…"

"Ok, but for the other part it's right?"

"Yes... So, music, many instruments working together to paint a picture with sounds. They need to work together to create the harmony. Their vibrations need to match, and when they do, we have music..."

"Yes, I follow your thought, continue..."

"Then could the same be said if people worked together and created their own peaceful vibration, and created harmony with others, would those vibrations have a good impact in and on this world?"

"Yes, it would. Vibrations tend to affect each other. And when in harmony, they enhance each other. When in disharmony, they work against each other."

"Thought you said that disharmony was perspective and preference?"

"No, but sounding awful is, and sounding awful is what you said, because we do mark words exactly, don't we?"

"I cannot reply anything else than yes on that after the ears comment."

"Thought not, good ol' Roy!"

Music in reality

The likeness with music is far more brilliant than Roy thought. Because not only does each frequency affect others and is affected by others, but it is also a multiversal law that what frequencies send out is what they attract.

Thus, a person in harmony, a group of people in harmony, a world in harmony, all attract harmony. And vice versa, any disharmony attracts other disharmonies. Which can be observed all over, in big and small. In people and in nature.

Point being, you can influence your surroundings in different ways, by the way you act, by your choices, by the way you are and how you interact with others as well as nature. Even if this might sound like religious beliefs, it is a scientific mechanism behind it, and even if that mechanism wasn't discovered or had been put to words at this stage in this world, things are the way they are even if it is unspoken.

This being said, to connect back to a previous dialogue, when you do things that makes you feel good, and is 'right', it works as a good force in the multiverse, and disharmonies creates, well, I'm sure you get it...

Laughter according to Roy

"Then I wonder, or rather, I have formed another theory."

"Let's hear it!"

"Laughter!"

"Yes, what about it?"

"Before I continue, I assume, and this is part of the theory, that laughter is not only something that exists in this world? And I dare to answer it myself and say that it is multiversal?"

"I'd say it is, but I really have never thought about it."

"You and I have laughed a great deal together today, and I am a being of this world, whilst you are a being of the multiverse, yet laughter is a common language for the both of us, despite us having very different points of references."

"So far, everything checks out."

"Another question before I continue, we do speak the same language, how come?"

"I speak every language of every corner of the multiverse…"

"It figures, anyway, in this newly formed theory of mine, I claim that laughter is essential to life. And I will also claim that it is not only essential to life, it is also the glue that keeps things together, body, soul, mind and life essence… mind, will, thoughts and feelings… it is something that affects everything and everybody with its effects… and all living beings need it and long for it and can be infected by it, and it can spread wide and fast… it can even be communicated over time and distance through written or spoken words."

"This far, no argument from me!"

"Does that mean it is true?"

"Not necessarily, and to be honest, no not really, but only flawed by details, not general concept."

"Ok, but then let's ignore those details for a while."

"Will do!"

"Now, if laughter is something that binds everything together, then is not laughter the key to everything? Laughter can get us closer to the multiversal forces, closer to ourselves, closer to others, get in touch with life itself through the bridge of laughter?"

"To my knowledge it has never been used that way, and no one, again, to my knowledge, has ever attempted using laughter as a key to anything before."

"Then perhaps I will be the first one."

"A little something, if I may, something that I probably should not say, but still, I relay this message through you, and it is meant for two different people that you will encounter. Should you figure out which two people, everything may change dramatically, and if not, no harm done, things will be what they'll be…"

"Ok, what is the message then?"

"What you just said about laughter…"

"But that was something I said, how can that be your message to some other people? And how will I know who to deliver this message to?"

"I will not tell you, because I've already said too much, but I can give you a clue. There are very few people who will not take you for a mad man when you speak about things like this. And the message is probably to two of those people."

"Then it is easy, I'll just say it to anyone I meet, then I am sure to have delivered your message to the right people."

"Indeed, you'll have done just that, if that is your approach, but using that strategy will also mean you have told the wrong people about it. And that has severe consequences for a great deal of people, not only in this world, but in other worlds as well…"

"So, you lay upon me to deliver a message from you, that was really not from you, it was my words, twice, to people I do not know who, and should I deliver the message to the wrong people, it is devastating, but if I deliver to the right persons it will be tremendously great?"

"Yes, something like that!"

"Oh, ok, thank you I guess, what a lousy favour to ask for!"

Laughter in reality

Laughter is truly multiversal, a language that everybody understands, every living thing, every living creature. But laughter takes very different forms in different beings. When one creature laughs another creature can interpret it as hostility. So, not even one of the most common things in the multiverse will make it easier for people to meet and get along. Then, on the other hand, the construction of the multiverse is with multiple, natural barriers that cannot, and in some cases should not, be forced or breached.

How will I know who according to Roy

"Sometimes things are the way they are just by chance, sometimes things are the way they are for a reason."

"Perhaps, but this does not help me in any way, nor does it relieve me of a great responsibility. If I screw up, there are serious consequences, if I succeed, there are great benefits… so at this point I am inclined to do nothing, which seems the best option right now."

"I have not been completely honest in giving you the full picture. See it like this. You've been tasked with a mission, should you give the information to the wrong people, the multiverse will face one of its biggest setbacks since it started to exist. This world will face dark times no matter what, do nothing and it is not given path on what will happen, how or when the dark ages will end, so to speak. Should you on the other hand succeed in giving it to the right persons, and only the right persons, this world will flourish and recover well from the darkness. And in the long run, it will not only be this world that benefits from that outcome."

"Then you'll have to get me something more to go on than who it might feel natural to share those kinds of thoughts with who will not see me as a nut case!"

"Well, really, I do not need to do anything, I can just sit back, watch and enjoy the show. But what you might be asking me is what I *choose* to do, and if I can choose to do anything other than I have already communicated to be my choice."

"What?"

"I think you are asking me to make a different choice and tell you something more, even if I have already said that I will not say anything more."

"Yeah, something like that."

"Then ask me something, see if I choose to answer it."

"Can't you just bloody tell me how it is that I am supposed to deliver your message to?"

"No."

"Then you have to… then I want you to make a different choice. I need you to make a different choice!"

"Is that because you do not want to make a difficult choice yourself?"

"Yes, I do not want to make a choice regarding this, it is too much at stake. I feel that I cannot be responsible for something this big and important."

"Does it help you if I say that this is nothing compared to what you will have to choose in your future?"

"No, not really, and it almost makes me not wanting to face anymore futures."

"You just need to trust me on this."

"I have no choice in this, have I?"

"We always have a choice, Roy, that is the whole point. Sadly, we do not always have every piece of information to make the best choice."

"Then what information will you share to make my choice easier?"

"Well, I can tell you this much, to get the most benefits out of it, you need to make it a chain reaction. And this is tricky. The information will need to reach one person who you've met and trust deeply, the other person is someone you've never met yet, and who will earn your trust much later than when this piece of information has had the possibility to make difference. Also, and this is important, the information cannot reach certain people, among them Groll."

"But Groll is dying, I will not have the possibility to tell him this…"

"Not now, you won't, but keep that in mind, it is of high importance that Groll never finds this out. Nor Rueen, come to think of it."

"Ok, I don't understand how I am supposed to be able to tell them, but I'll keep that in mind!"

"And there are two more things I choose to share with you. The first being that there are people around you that will trick you to earn your trust, or the trust of people you trust, possibly to gain this piece of information or other information that you, and you alone, are in possession of, so be careful!"

"And the other thing?"

"This is trickier to explain. But in order to get the information to the right people, without risking it getting to the wrong people, you need to deliver the information in the right time, to the right people, and the right people not being those who need to get the information. If you deliver it too late, dangerous, too early, even more dangerous, and just as a courtesy I will tell you that one of the two people you need to entrust this information to, in order to see to it that it gets to the right people is by sharing it to someone you do not trust."

"And this is my mission?"

"Yes, this is your mission. And you need to carry it out with precision and great care in order for it to succeed!"

"Mission impossible, I would say!"

"No way, this is a hunt you will master, no matter how dark the odds are!"

"Is this something you know or something you say to make me feel better?"

"Not something I know, I can only say that this is one of many possible outcomes from this point on."

How will I know who in reality

A tricky mission, or task, but not an impossible one. And at this point, it was certainly a confusing task for Roy, because he lacked perspective that he would gain with time, not counting chronologically, but time as it passed to Roy, including his different occasional time-jumps.

And the sad truth behind it all is that, whoever we are, we do never have all the pieces of the puzzle when we make critical decisions. There are always more than meets the eye, as Groll used to say.

And at this point in time, I cannot say whether it all played out as the Wizard tasked Roy to carry out, or if there was any other outcome of that part of the conversation. The only thing I with certainty can say is that this whole conversation between Roy and the Wizard did have plenty of positive impact on many worlds in the multiverse, not just the one we currently focus our attention on.

But all and all, the strange and a little incomprehensive clues that the Wizard chose to share with Roy on that mountainside that day did partly help Roy in completing his given task. And the biggest challenge was not, as Roy first thought, to deliver the right information to the right people in the right time, but to keep it from the wrong people trough out time and history. And wise from his experience with trying to cover the tracks of Atlantis he struggled greatly not to make a big deal of laughter or think of his theory regarding it. But as we all know, the more we try not to think of anything, the harder it gets not to think of it. Like if I would say: Don't think about a pink elephant, then most people will think of a pink elephant. And those who struggle with it may accomplish just thinking of an ordinary elephant, without the pink colour. Very few people manage to think of something completely different. And Roy is one of those who, when is asked NOT to think of a pink elephant, thinks of a pink elephant. Thus, this being one of his greatest challenges throughout his long life. And being immortal, it is a very long one.

Well, I am sorry, now I am rambling on again, but the close we get to the end, the more time I want to spend with you, and the more I want to tell you. But I know that if you chose to follow the stories of this world, you will learn more eventually, even if it is not me who will tell you the story directly. But I can assure you of one thing that might already be obvious, you have not seen or heard the last of Roy. He will accompany you further on this journey, and I don't know how you feel, but to me it is good to know that at least some of the travelling companions are some one that I know in advance. To me, it makes the journey more enjoyable to share with friends, even if the journey itself is a good hotbed for making new friends.

Well, enough about the rambling and onward with the story, it has not ended just yet!

Changing perspectives according to Roy and in reality

"All this makes me dizzy, and for the moment I will pretend I have not heard it and come back to it later on, let it sink in for a while.

"That is quite alright!"

"Another thing, I have been thinking a lot about perspective throughout our conversation."

"What about it? There is an infinite amount of perspectives on perspective."

"Since perspective can change, and often needs to change, the most important thing a human being can do is to keep an open mind. And settle for that right here, right now, this is what I know, this is how I understand things. But also, being aware that there are several more ways to look at it, and the perspective is never complete. Thus, if a human being is in a place or situation where everything feels heavy and dull, all it would take is a change of perspective to ease the burden."

"I am following you so far…"

"Then I will connect back to the beginning of our conversation, being miserable is a choice, being happy is a choice. Each and every situation and state of mind is a choice. Perspective and choice are connected in a way."

"Quite right, dear Roy! But it is hard for most to see it that way. There is many that are stuck in the victim's role in life. Always blaming someone or something else for their situation. But there is a way out of that using your mind and change your perspective."

"If I could teach everybody that, there would be much less pain and sorrow in the world."

"Indeed, but it is very easy to think and understand the concept of changing perspective. A whole other thing to live by it. Take Groll, he is fully aware of all this. Yet, when Rueen died, he did not choose to lose his faith in humanity, nor choose to be sad for ages. It happened to him, and even with the knowledge, he had not the strength or the energy to do something about it. It was a choice he in theory could have made, but in reality, was unable to do."

"There is a difference of knowing the path and walking it…"

"Very true!"

"But still, it would be a good thing to teach everybody… Getting everybody the tools to live a life fully by their own choice, in all matters…"

"I admire you for even considering doing that, should you choose to pursuit it, it will be a hard and difficult journey for you, might even lead to your own death, but you would affect this world in far greater ways than you could ever imagine!"
"I am thinking maybe I could use a life cycle to do this, then disappear and start over, but not pursuit that anymore, put my hope to the message itself, and let the message live and spread."

"Could be done… if planned carefully…"

"Yes, but not yet, I have other matters to attend to in a little while."

The Goodbye according to Roy

"That you do, and now it's time for me. I need to get going, to say goodbye to an old friend."

"Then I guess it is soon time for me to go as well."

"Indeed, it is... This has been a pleasure. I have enjoyed it much!"

"Do I see you again?"

"You have had a habit of doing so in the past, something tells me that you will keep that habit."

"Then I guess this is not goodbye for us, only see you later!"

"Something like that."

"I have also enjoyed this. You have given me quite a bit to think about. Almost wish I had another eternity to digest it all before I head back to Dee and the others."

"To my surprise, you have given me a thing or two to think about as well... and I am sure that you will notice one thing really soon."

"Riddles from the Wiseard... If you have taught me one thing is that I need to be patient with you and the things you say... but I am pleased about the 'really soon' part. Even if I have no way of telling if it is soon in my perspective or yours. Either way it could still be ages away, or not."

"...more like 'or not'..."

"Thank you, old friend."

"Thank you as well, dear Roy!"

"See you later!"

"And you! And an advice along the way..."

"What?"

"Don't mention me to others, I guess it takes your mind to almost wrap around this, I anticipate that almost all others will deem you crazy and untrustworthy."

"More than they already do when I tell them I am an immortal?"

"Something like that... and another thing… dress warm, there will be a shift in weather shortly!"

The Goodbye in reality

The reality in it, from the Wizards perspective, was that one of his oldest friends on this world were about to leave it. He would miss Groll, and even if Roy, or anybody else, can't act as a replacement for anyone else, it is still good to know you have a friend.

Roy did not know this at the time but became aware of it over time. And this suited Roy as well, both had someone to share memories of Groll and Rueen, and time that had passed. Changing perspective. Challenging perspective. Because Roy did something Groll never had done, Roy challenged the Wizard with his very unique point of view. Mostly because of genuine curiosity, but also by active choice. And the Wizard appreciated this equally much.

Things Roy said or asked often had consequences throughout the multiverse or on one of its many worlds, not only Roy's own world.

So, it was never a goodbye. And in a way, it never is, with anyone.

The storyteller in reality

Now, as you are getting close to the last page of this book, you might wonder who has been tagging along for the entire book, sharing things in between, adding and changing things as we have moved along from chapter to chapter and story to story.

I am going to give you time to let the question sink in and give you a little background to relate to.

All in all, you have met two characters in this book. One is already stated in the title: 'The amazing adventures of Roy Hicks', and the other is a Wizard, of the four Wizards acting in the multiverse.

Then of course a number of other people that have appeared in the stories. But those are to be considered side characters supporting the two main roles in this.

One main character, Roy, could say to be self-centred, egoistic and not very truthful at times. Not that he has lied with the intention of harming anyone, but only to entertain and build a great story.

The other main character, who does not appear in the tile of the book is a very odd creature, and hard for any human to wrap his or her mind around.

If you think about it, it is just Roy and the Wizard who were present during the dialog on the mountain, where this entire book has taken place, not counting the various stories that are set in a different location.
You may also have noticed that there is no chapter called 'The storyteller according to Roy'.

Adding up these facts, you might get a clue as to who I am.

If not, I will give you one last piece of information that will make your odds 50/50 in at least guessing. It is either Roy or the Wizard that have commented in between.

As for Roy, it could be a chance to rectify the lies in the story and a chance to deliver a more balanced version of what really took place.

As for the Wizard, it could be a chance to continue to show his knowledge and wisdom and adding a few extra perspectives that are important for communicating the whole story with every side represented.

It is either one of us that are the mystery voice in between, and once you know the answer who wrote this, you will probably have a pretty good idea as to why there is no chapter called 'The storyteller according to Roy'.

Now it is time for me to round off this chapter, and with it, ending this book. But this is not farewell, we will meet again, if you wish it.

So, time for the last words, and still no revealing identity. If your eyes have leaped forward, you might have seen my ending initials already. Made you look right away, didn't I?

Last sentence before me signing off this chapter and ending the book.

Yours truly,
RH